PELICAN BOOKS
A656

CHECK YOUR OWN I.Q.

Dr H. J. Eysenck, who was born in 1916, obtained his Ph.D. degree in psychology at London University after school and university experience in Germany, France, and England. Having worked as psychologist at the war-time Mill Hill Emergency Hospital, he was appointed Professor of Psychology in the University of London, and Director of the Psychological Department at the Institute of Psychiatry (Maudsley and Bethlem Royal Hospitals). He has lectured in many countries, and been Visiting Professor at the Universities of Pennsylvania and of California. Known mainly through his experimental researches in the field of personality, he has written some three hundred articles in technical journals, as well as several books including *Dimensions of Personality*, *The Scientific Study of Personality*, *The Structure of Human Personality*, *The Psychology of Politics*, *The Dynamics of Anxiety and Hysteria*, *Uses and Abuses of Psychology*, *Sense and Nonsense in Psychology*, *Crime and Personality*, *Fact and Fiction in Psychology*, *The Biological Base of Personality*, and *Description and Measurement of Personality*. He has also edited a *Handbook of Abnormal Psychology*, two volumes of *Experiments in Personality*, and *Behaviour Therapy and the Neuroses*. He is Editor-in-Chief of the journal *Behaviour Research and Therapy*. He advocates the highest degree of scientific rigour in the design of psychological experiments and is very critical of much loose thinking current at present under the guise of 'psychology'. *Know Your Own I.Q.*, a Pelican which was the first book to permit the reader to determine his own I.Q., was published in 1962 and has been reprinted several times.

H. J. EYSENCK

CHECK YOUR OWN

I.Q.

PENGUIN BOOKS

Penguin Books Ltd, Harmondsworth, Middlesex, England
Penguin Books Australia Ltd, Ringwood, Victoria, Australia

—

First published 1966
Reprinted 1967, 1968

—

Copyright © H. J. Eysenck, 1966

—

Made and printed in Great Britain
by C. Nicholls & Company Ltd
Set in Monotype Times

CONTENTS

INTRODUCTION

Know Your Own I.Q., which was published in Pelican Books in 1962, had the distinction of being top of the best-seller list for a while, which seemed good evidence that the assumption made in preparing it was justified, to wit, that most people are interested in the measurement of intelligence, would like to find out more about it, and would like to see, under actual test conditions, what sort of thing an 'intelligence test' really is. Many people may complain that intelligence tests are too much with us, night and day; however, they have come to stay, and it is likely that better use will be made of them if it is more widely understood what they can and cannot do than when they are regarded as either instruments of the Devil or inviolable tools of science.

The Introduction to *Know Your Own I.Q.* discussed in some detail the nature of intelligence tests, but the large number of letters written in response to the publication of that book indicated that it left many questions unanswered, and the Introduction to this new book seems an excellent place to answer some of these questions. The main part of the book, of course, consists of tests; many of these are similar to the ones in *Know Your Own I.Q.*, but some are rather different. Before turning to the questions a brief explanation of why these additional tests have been included will be in order.

The eight tests in *Know Your Own I.Q.* were all what are sometimes called *omnibus* tests; in other words they were measures of general intelligence which used verbal, numerical, and pictorial material indiscriminately, and also used many different ways of presenting the problem. In this way one hopes to cancel out specific abilities and disabilities; thus a person who is good with problems involving words, but poor with problems involving numbers, will find both equally represented, and is thus neither handicapped nor favoured. The first five tests of this book are similar in type and give an overall estimate of the reader's I.Q., provided instructions are faithfully followed.

However, the reader may wish to know a little more about his specific abilities and disabilities, and for that purpose we have included three separate tests dealing with three special abilities. These are called verbal, numerical, and visuo-spatial, and while one would expect one *omnibus* test to give results pretty similar to another one for the same person, it is quite on the cards that the same person will do well on one of these three special tests, poorly on a second, and average on the third. There are, of course, many more such special strengths and weaknesses than can be measured by three tests, but these are probably the most important and most widely recognized ones. The inclusion should add interest to the book, as well as giving the reader more information about his mental abilities than he would get from a simple I.Q. The I.Q. is a mere average, and it is often more important to have separate measures of the things which are being averaged, than to know what the average is.

We have also added a few sets of problems playfully called 'Limbering Up for Intellectual Giants'. These originated because many readers wrote to say that surely the kind of problem included in ordinary intelligence tests was much too easy to be an accurate measure of their own splendid and far-reaching intellectual ability; would not something more difficult and complicated be more appropriate? Well, here is something more difficult, which may keep them busy for many long evenings; it would not, unfortunately, be more appropriate because, from the very nature of things, such problems cannot, and do not, lend themselves very easily to the calculation of an I.Q. These problems are, therefore, given simply for the amusement of finding the right solution; to translate scores into I.Q.s would have been misleading. Reasons why this is so will be given a little later.

Now let us turn to some of the questions posed. The first of these, and much the most widely repeated, dealt with the problem of alternative answers. In tones of anger or sorrow, of scorn or of commiseration, many readers pointed out that many problems have alternative answers thought up by themselves. Some readers tried to elucidate the theoretical principles on the basis of which a choice between different answers could be made; others declared the whole thing a fraud and a delusion.

Curiously enough there is very little scientific work on this problem, although it has been with us ever since the first intelligence tests were constructed. Perhaps it may help if we look first of all at the question of when precisely alternative answers occur. We can present an I.Q. problem in two main ways. One way is not only to present the problem, but also a number of alternative solutions; when this is done it is easy to make sure that all these alternatives are decisively wrong, except for the correct one. Even here there are certain premises which are not usually stated but which are understood by all. One of these premises, which is very important indeed, is that all the information given in the problem should be used, and that a solution which does this is superior to another solution which only makes use of part of the information. However, there is never any real difficulty about problems presented in this manner, unless the person who sets the test is careless, or unless the proof-reader lets an error go through unchecked.

There is, however, another type of problem where the person who does the test is not given one correct, and several indubitably incorrect solutions, but where he has to think out the solution independently; this is sometimes called an 'open' problem. There are degrees of 'openness', ending up with a type of problem where there simply is not one correct solution but a very large number, and where the intelligence of the testee is shown by the number of correct answers he supplies in a given time. Let us take an open problem and see what kind of principles we can discover. Here is the problem:

A dwarf lives on the twentieth floor of a skyscraper. Every morning he goes into the lift, pushes the correct button, and is taken to the ground floor; he goes off to work and comes back in the evening. He enters the lift, pushes the button, and goes up to the tenth floor; he then walks up the rest of the stairs. The question is: Why doesn't he go up to the twentieth floor in the lift?

You might like to try and answer this question yourself, and you might like to give it to other people. Some of the more frequent answers you will get are:

'He does it for the exercise'; or

'Because he wants to lose weight'; or

'He visits a friend on the tenth floor'.

('Mistress' is sometimes substituted for 'friend' by extraverted subjects.)

Now these and many other reasons are perfectly possible; why are they wrong, and why is the correct solution, namely that he cannot reach higher than the tenth button, right? The answer, of course, is simply that the wrong answers don't take into account all the elements of the problem; they would apply to a giant just as much as to a dwarf. Obviously the solution must involve the fact that the man in the lift is a dwarf – otherwise why bother to say so. This is, of course, not a very good problem for an intelligence test, but you can see why out of many solutions which are more or less correct (because they take into account some of the elements of the problem) one, and only one, is in fact counted as correct. In this case, it is pretty obvious which of the alternatives is the right solution, but sometimes people might feel disposed to argue the point. Let us consider another problem, this time of the 'find the odd man out' kind. Here are five towns, and you are required to pick the odd man out. The towns are Panama, London, Duluth, Cambridge, and Edsele.

Now each of these places could be considered the odd man out several times over on a variety of grounds. Edsele is the only town east of Greenwich, while Panama is the only town where vowels alternate with consonants. Cambridge is the only town housing world famous universities on both sides of the Atlantic. Duluth is the only town ending in -th. You might go on to pick out the one town that was farthest north, or farthest south, or west, or that had the largest number of people in it, or the smallest. In other words, the number of ways in which one town can stand out, as it were, from the others and be considered 'odd man out' is very large. Nevertheless the correct solution will have been quite obvious to most people; it is, of course, Cambridge because all the other towns have only one single vowel which is repeated several times in each, whereas Cambridge has three different vowels.

Why is this solution 'better' than any of the others? To say that the reason is intuitively obvious would probably be true, but does not get us very far. To put it into words one might perhaps say something like this. You have been set a problem. This problem must contain all the information required to solve it, and the person setting it must clearly have selected the five constituent words in a very careful manner such that conjointly they point to a unique right answer. Now in any set of five towns, one must be the biggest, one the smallest, one the farthest north, one the farthest south, one the one with the largest number of letters, one the one with the smallest number of letters; no unique solution can be achieved along these lines because they would apply to any quite accidental choice of town. But there is something clearly unique and non-accidental in the fact that in four towns out of five all the vowels in each word are identical; this would not happen by chance once in a million times, and must, therefore, be intentional. It follows that the answer given above as correct stands out from all the others because it makes use of an item of information in the test which is not used at all by the other alternative answers.

One point is interesting in this connexion, and that is that very intelligent people often realize what is the required answer (which is quite obvious to them from the beginning) but go on searching for an alternative with which to confound the setter of the problem. In other words they regard the solving of an intelligence test as a kind of intellectual gladiatorial combat in which they are one point up if they find a genuine alternative answer overlooked by the setter. (This attitude fortunately seems to vanish when something important is at stake, such as the 11-plus examination; under those conditions, even the most highly intelligent seem to be content with the mundane 'correct' answers so clearly demanded by the problems.)

There are other indications of what is the 'correct solution', which simply looking at a single problem may not bring to light. Thus in many types of intelligence test a particular kind of solution is developed very early, and in terms of that solution easy and unambiguous items lead later to more complex and ambiguous ones. Part of the intelligence which is being tested consists in applying what one should have learned in doing the easier problems to the more difficult ones. It is always possible for the critic then to pick out one of the later items, flourish it indignantly in the air, and ask: 'Why is the solution given by the author of the test correct and this other one incorrect?' Test items should no more be used out of their context than quotations; what went before may be very important in evaluating what comes later. A test is a unit and cannot arbitrarily be broken up.

There are many other considerations which determine why one answer is right and another one not, and the reader may have some fun in trying to find for himself the logical principles involved. Here I would add only one point which I think is very important. The arguments I have given so far may strike the reader as reasonable, but to the psychologist even a reasonable argument does not appeal as much as an experimental demonstration. What is usually done in test construction, therefore, is this. You give the whole test to a sample of say 1,000 people; you then assign a total score to each of these, on the basis of their performance. Next you look at all those items, of which there will be only a few in any given test, where alternative answers are possible with some show of reason. Then, picking out the brightest quarter of the sample and the dullest quarter of the sample, the psychologist would study the actual answers given by these two groups. However certain he may be that answer A is better than answer B, he would throw out the item unless he found that answer A was actually given much more frequently by the brighter group than by the duller one, and answer B by the duller group than by the brighter one. This process is sometimes called *item analysis*, and is a very important adjunct to the original selection of items; it makes certain that the psychologist in setting the test does not incorporate unfortunate idiosyncrasies of his own which might prove a handicap to some people and a help to others.

But why, some people may ask, bother with 'open' items of any kind, where with all your care and item analysis we may still overlook certain possibilities? Some psychologists go along with this objection and only use closed items where this possibility does not arise. This solution obviates any criticism based on the possibility of alternative answers, but it raises other difficulties. If the I.Q. is an average, and if the form of the question is an important element which favours some people and puts others off, then by restricting oneself to just one type of question, one may unwittingly bias the average in one direction or the other. The 11-plus examination, by concentrating very much on 'closed' questions, has possibly resulted in favouring the non-original, non-productive, bureaucratic, and civil service type of intelligence, while penalizing the original, creative, scientific, and artistic type of mentality. This criticism has been made by American workers who have had a great deal of experience with 'open' tests, and who have found that children who do particularly well at 'open' tests may not do so well at 'closed' ones, and vice versa. I do not think that the evidence is conclusive on this point, but I would not be surprised at all if there were not a good deal of truth in it. However that may be, it is certainly unwise in the absence of definite knowledge on the point to concentrate entirely on one type of question; the only safe course is to have as wide a variety as possible. If this can only be done at the risk of occasionally being wrongly (or even rightly) accused of setting a problem having alternative answers, then I think the risk is worth taking.

Another criticism which was made by many correspondents related to the requirement for specific knowledge involved in certain test items. Recalling that I have, myself, distinguished carefully between intelligence and knowledge, they queried the admissibility of items requiring specific knowledge in an intelligence test. The answer to this point goes roughly along these lines. The measurement of intelligence obviously requires certain fundamental elements of knowledge, motivation, habit, and experience in common among testees. Obviously you could not begin to do the problems in this book if you could not read, did not know how to hold a pencil, were blind, did not know the meaning of elementary English words, or were not motivated to undergo the task at all. All these points present problems in comparing the intelligence of one social, national, or ethnic group with another. Some working-class children still have genuine problems in holding a pencil, or in laboriously making marks on paper; this may interfere with their test-taking ability. If the test contains words like 'cow' or 'ship', there is even now some indication that city children are handicapped more than children of rural or coastal environments. Comparisons between white and Red Indian groups can be totally invalidated by different sets. Thus white children easily respond to the instruction that they should not worry too much about errors, or about leaving the problem unsolved and going on to the next one. The Red Indian on the other hand is brought up by his tribe in the belief that it is far more important to be right than to be quick; consequently he is quite likely to get stuck early on in the test, and to refuse to leave the problem which is giving him difficulty, thus relinquishing the opportunity of earning more points by solving other, possibly simpler problems.

To obtain a reasonable measure, therefore, we must have a certain homogeneity of motivation, background training, set, experience, and knowledge; no intelligence test is universally valid, but applies only to a given sub-section of the population. *Know Your Own I.Q.*, as well as the present book, was intended for literate, English-speaking people, between the ages of eighteen and fifty or sixty, with above average I.Q.s and a corresponding minimum degree of schooling. Given such a fairly homogeneous group, it has been shown that knowledge is a direct function of I.Q., as determined by tests not involving specific items of knowledge. Simple vocabulary tests for instance have been found to be the single best index of intelligence, and indeed it does not seem unreasonable that knowledge of a person's native language should be related to his intellectual ability; after all, the chances of acquiring a good vocabulary are limited more by lack of intellectual ability than by outside restrictions. This general rule, of course, does not necessarily apply to groups other than that for which *Know Your Own I.Q.* and the present book are intended, but within that group it was thought highly likely that the inclusion of a few questions involving specific knowledge would increase the validity of the I.Q. obtained. If one's purpose were to compare different social groups, or different nations, or different ethnic groups, then, of course, one would have to take great care to eliminate items of this type.

Another point about which many people wrote is concerned with the actual definition and meaning of the term 'intelligence'. They found it unsatisfactory to be left up in the air with a statement, however true, that psychologists were not agreed upon the theoretical interpretation, even though they all used quite similar types of intelligence tests. Now a demand to know what it is that you are measuring, as well as knowing how to measure it, is not unreasonable, and I shall try here to say a few words about the nature of intelligence, as measured by intelligence tests. Before doing so, however, I want to make it clear that what I am saying is my own interpretation of the facts, based on a knowledge of the literature and many years of experimental work in this field; what I have to say will not necessarily be endorsed by other psychologists, and may, of course, be quite mistaken. However, there is a good chance that the truth may lie somewhere in this direction.

When we analyse performance on intelligence tests in some detail, we find that there is one outstanding characteristic which more than any other determines success or failure. This characteristic is mental speed. If you take a number of quite simple problems, all of the same type – say a letter series, e.g. A, C, E, G? – then you find that hardly anyone will make an error, or find the problems too difficult, but some people will solve a set of twenty or thirty of these problems in a few seconds, while others take almost as many minutes over it. Now it has been shown that these differences in speed are carried over into more and more difficult problems; in other words those who are quick on the easy ones are also quick with more and more difficult problems, while those who are slow on the easy ones are also slow on the difficult ones. This all-pervasive mental speed, I would say, is the fundamental, inherited basis for intellectual differences among people.

This speed factor, however, is not identical with I.Q. This is due to the fact that in any particular I.Q. test various non-intellectual personality factors also come into play. Let us first make sure that speed is indeed an important variable in the typical I.Q. test. You will probably find that even though you cannot do more than a few of the problems in the half-hour which you are allotted, you can, if you are willing to persevere long enough, do practically all the problems in each set. Thus the time restriction on the test is essential, as otherwise almost everybody could get a perfect score. It is this which makes a more complex and difficult test item impossible to include in a typical test of intelligence; if you look at the tests in our 'Limbering Up for Intellectual Giants' section, you will see that the kind of time limit we would have to give would be of the nature of several hours or even days, and administratively and practically this is simply not feasible.

In actual fact people would not get perfect scores, even if given unlimited time. This is due to certain personality factors which interfere with performance in the long run, and often do so even in the short run. The two main personality features which have been experimentally studied and identified in this connexion may be called by their popular names, carelessness and lack of persistence. If you are slow, then a test which the quick-witted may complete successfully in half an hour may take you twenty hours; your enthusiasm may wane before the time is up, and you may give up and regard certain problems as insoluble even though you might have solved them if you had gone on a little longer. This lack of persistence, of course, also affects performance over very much shorter periods; some people are willing to spend half a minute on a problem, but not two minutes. In fact there seems to be a logarithmic relationship between difficulty-level of item and length of time required to solve it; this makes the demands on the persistence of the relatively slow-witted very much greater than would otherwise be the case; nevertheless there is a possibility, particularly in ordinary life, but also in tests with a liberal time allowance, of trading persistence for speed of mental functioning; you can make up on the swings what you lose on the roundabouts. (And, of course, you can lose on the swings what nature has kindly provided you with on the roundabouts!)

Even if you are quick-witted and persistent, you might nevertheless be slapdash and careless, accepting the first idea that comes into your head without checking to see whether the solution is in fact correct or not. Malfunctioning of the 'error-checking mechanism' leads to poor marks just as inexorably as does slow speed of mental functioning and as does lack of persistence; extraverted people tend to be rather poorer in this respect, and to make more errors than do introverts. There is also some good evidence to indicate that people who are original and creative (and therefore good at 'open' tests) tend to make careless errors in 'closed' tests; this may be another reason for reopening the question of whether the 11-plus examination is not unfair to certain types of intellects.

This then in outline is the kind of picture of the problem-solving mechanism which appears to be called for to account for the facts in our possession; it was originally suggested by Mr D. Furneaux whose outstanding work on university student selection has led him more and more in the direction of emphasizing the importance of personality in the measurement of what purports to be a purely intellectual function. In so far as the I.Q. is a purely intellectual measure, it is a measure of mental speed; but I.Q. inevitably is not a pure measure of mental speed unless very careful precautions are taken to make it so. In the ordinary way the measure of mental speed is adulterated by the intrusion of personality features such as persistence, or lack of it, and carelessness or carefulness. These personality features are probably much more subject to training than is mental speed, although even there Skinner, the well-known American psychologist who has done so much to popularize teaching machines, has shown that you can actually increase dramatically the speed with which intelligence test problems are solved, by a suitable course on a teaching machine programmed to deal with problems of this type. He also found, and this is in good accord with the analysis given above, that with a properly programmed course of instruction, even the dullest, most slow-witted, could succeed as well as the brightest, most quick-witted, but that they took inordinately more time over the work. It has been found, for instance, that some very quick-witted students, working on a properly programmed mathematics course, could do a year's work in something like two days! It is indeed one of the great advantages of the teaching machine that it enables every student to go at his own pace, which is governed largely, of course, by his mental speed, but also by personality features, accidents of his up-bringing, special abilities, and so on; to force everyone to go at the same speed, as is inevitable with a single human instructor, is obviously a much less successful method and is bound to lead to difficulties, both for the very quick and the very slow.

If all this sounds too much like common sense, and is too devoid of that fearsome jargon in which even the most elementary facts of psychology are usually wrapped up, the reader will have to make allowances. In any case by looking back over his own performance on the tests, taking into account the number of wrong answers and problems begun but not finished, he will be able to get a rough idea at least of his own standing with regard to these three factors of mental speed, persistence, and error checking.

I just mentioned Skinner, and his demonstration that speed of problem solving could be increased by suitable practice. This brings up another question often asked. Many readers complained indignantly that in *Know Your Own I.Q.* they had a score of 110 on the first test, 116 on the second, 120 on the third, and even higher ones later. How, they ask quite reasonably, can their I.Q. have changed within a few days by such considerable amounts? The answer, of course, is, as I pointed out in *Know Your Own I.Q.*, that intelligence tests are subject to practice and coaching effects, and that these may add, on the usual type of test, something like ten points of I.Q. from first to fifth test or so. (After the fifth test there is probably no increase in I.Q., and even from the third to the fifth test there is relatively little. Most of the increase occurs after the first test.) There is no doubt that this is a serious drawback as far as intelligence tests are concerned, and it was one of my purposes in writing the book to bring it to everybody's attention. There is obviously a considerable injustice in subjecting children, at an important stage of their scholastic career, to a test of intelligence when some have never seen such a test before while others have had a good deal of practice on tests.

Regardless of the question of the 11-plus examination, this is a point on which one may rightly feel rather uneasy. There is little doubt that mental testing will be used more and more widely, both with children and with adults, at school, at university, in the armed forces, and in industry. It is essential that tests should be fair, and should be seen to be fair, if this increase in intelligence testing is not to raise more problems than it solves. Now an increase in performance, due to test sophistication, of, say, eight points may not seem much, but of course, in selection the only trouble that arises occurs in connexion with marginal candidates; if the crucial level for selection is an I.Q. of 115 then children with an I.Q. below 105 or thereabouts will probably not be competing anyway, and children with an I.Q. of 125 or over will probably win through under almost any conditions. The range of doubtful cases, therefore, would only cover some twenty points of I.Q., and compared with that a possible increase of eight points may quite frequently make all the difference between success and failure. The figures given do not, of course, pretend to any great accuracy, but they indicate the kind of problem which will so frequently be found in selection testing.

It might be preferable to keep everyone in ignorance of the nature of intelligence tests until the occasion for testing arises, but this is clearly impossible. In the first place, it would mean that everyone could only be tested once; having been tested at school he could never again approach an intelligence test with the necessary pristine ignorance. Furthermore, ways and means would have to be found for coaching to be declared illegal, and for children who had done the test to be sworn to secrecy. Printers, publishers, teachers, and psychologists would also have to sign the Official Secrets Act, and quite generally it would require an almost impossibly complicated system of inspection and enforcement to ensure anything like compliance with such a rule. And even if it were possible to ensure that the crucial test was always the first, I doubt very much if in fact this would be particularly desirable. There are many advantages in having several test results available, and following a child through school, watching the ups and downs of his intellectual growth, and relating them to his performance. Even if selection has to be made it would thus be possible to discover upswings in the I.Q. of the 'late developer', and redress an injustice that may have been done. I am, therefore, in favour of the alternative possibility, indicated above, which is to make everyone acquainted with I.Q. tests to a sufficient degree to reduce the effects of practice to an absolute minimum. I think it is a pity that psychologists have been remiss at drawing attention to this great defect in their measuring instruments and that they have not advocated ways and means of dealing with this difficulty. Lay people have often complained about this point, but have seldom received an answer from testing experts; the complaint is a very real one and a very important one and should not be glossed over. If it cannot be eradicated, then testing might be misleading and under certain circumstances worse than useless.

Readers below the age of eighteen or thereabouts, or above fifty-five to sixty, will tend to get lower scores than those of intermediate ages. Some readers have suggested that a table should be given which would enable subjects to calculate their appropriate I.Q.s, but this seems to be taking things a little too far. We can look at the I.Q. from an absolute or relative point of view. By absolute in this connexion I mean comparing one's own ability with that of the adult population as a whole; by relative in this connexion I mean comparing one's ability with that of others of the same age. It is obvious that if ability declines after the age of sixty, then a seventy-year-old will be handicapped when competing with a forty-year-old; thus in absolute terms his I.Q. is lower. In comparing his performance with that of another seventy-year-old it is likely that his relative standing will be much the same as it was when they were all forty; thus in a relative sense the seventy-year-old is not handicapped. While the estimation of a relative I.Q. has its use, of course, it has always struck me as being rather artificial and consequently no conversion tables are provided in this book; if older people want to claim a bonus they are, of course, welcome to do so. It is very difficult in any case to measure the appropriate size of the bonus as it is almost impossible to construct a reasonable sample of older people; so many of the people who should be in that sample have already passed away and are beyond measurement.

One last point. Many readers have said that they felt confused by two apparently contradictory opinions put forward in *Know Your Own I.Q.* and my previous Pelicans. On the one hand, they say, I put forward many serious criticisms of I.Q. measurement, which would make one mistrust profoundly any figure arrived at in this kind of test; on the other hand I claim that the selection process of the 11-plus testing is surprisingly accurate and valid. How can these statements be reconciled?

The answer is relatively simple, and it relates to the proper status of a psychologist in relation to social matters. Given that children are to be selected at a certain age for allocation to certain types of schools, in numbers decided in advance, and in order to succeed in programmes of study also decided in advance, then the educational psychologist who is given the task of constructing a selection programme is acting purely as a technologist. Given all these conditions, as well as the amount of money which is paid per head for the process of selection, and also the amount of money to be spent on research, one can only say that from this technological point of view, psychologists have been very successful. Thus the first part of my statement is, I think, undoubtedly justified.

However, the psychologist as a scientist may take issue with any or all of the things we have accepted above as 'given'. He may deny the desirability of selection, or of selection at a particular age, or for the particular purpose in hand. He may disagree with the proportions of children allocated to the various types of school, or even with the structure of the secondary schooling system. He may take issue with the kind of selection which is being practised, perhaps on the grounds that originality and creativity are excluded in favour of conformity, and he may declare that at the present stage of knowledge far too little money is spent on research. He may also come to the conclusion that while we are getting our testing done at bargain prices at the moment, it would be very much better for the future of our children if a much more thoroughgoing and long-continued system of psychological evaluation were employed. I think most psychologists would agree with some at least of these criticisms, even though they would agree that the technological aspects of modern selection were carried out very efficiently. The population at large unfortunately has always mistaken professional praise of technological work well done, for agreement on points which the technologist must take for granted; it is at this level that I would like to make the criticisms I have to make. However, this is not the place to discuss a topic as complex and fraught with emotion as is the 11-plus selection; the reader who has digested the facts provided in this and the previous Pelicans should be able to think about these issues on his own account.

INSTRUCTIONS

You have exactly thirty minutes to complete each of these tests. Don't linger too long over any item; you may be on the wrong track altogether, and might do better with the next one. On the other hand don't give up *too* easily; most of the problems can be worked out with a bit of patience. Just use your common sense in judging when to leave an item unsolved. And remember that on the whole items tend to get more difficult later in the test. Everybody should be able to do some items correctly, but nobody should be able to do all the items correctly in the time allowed.

Your answer in each case will consist of a single number, letter, or word. You may have to choose from various alternatives given to you, or you may have to think up the right answer. Indicate your answer clearly in the appropriate space. If you can't figure out the answer, don't guess; but if you have an idea but aren't quite sure if it is in fact the correct one, put it in. There are no 'trick' questions, but you should always consider a variety of ways of approaching the problem. Be sure you understand what is required of you before you start on a problem; you waste time if you go straight ahead without bothering to find out just what the problem is.

NOTE: Dots indicate the number of letters in a missing word; thus (. . . .) shows that the missing word you are required to find has four letters.

TEST ONE

1. Select the correct figure from the four numbered ones.

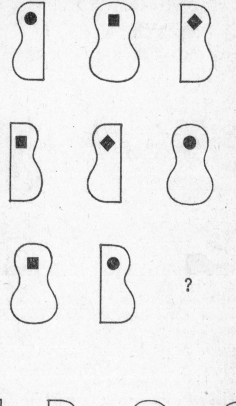

?

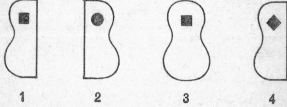

1   2   3   4

2. Insert the word that completes the first word and begins the second.

   PRACT (...) BERG

3. Find the odd man out:

   BLOW

   NOPOS

   LETAP

   DHATUMB

4. Insert the missing number.

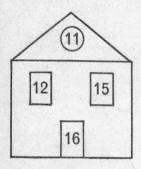 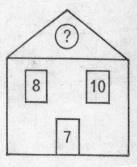

5. Insert the missing word.

   ORBIT (RILE) WHEEL

   ARSON (....) STEMS

6. Insert the missing number.

   196 (25) 324

   329 ( ) 137

7. What is the next number in the series?

   18   10   6   4   ?

8. Find the odd man out.

   BALET

   RACIH

   PATERC

   NACIMORA

9. Select the correct figure from the numbered ones.

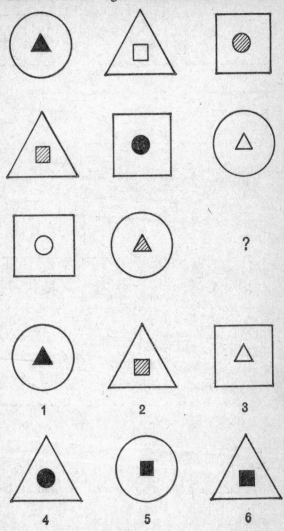

10. Select the correct figure from the six numbered ones.

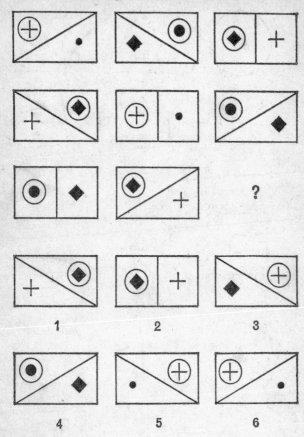

11. Insert the missing letter.

W T P M I ?

12. Insert the word that completes the first word and begins the second.

SHR (. . .) LING

13. Insert the missing number.

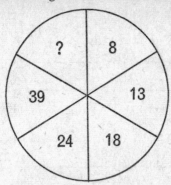

14. Insert the missing number.
    4   9   20
    8   5   14
    10   3   ?

15. Insert the missing number.
    16 (27) 43
    29 (   ) 56

16. Insert the missing letters.

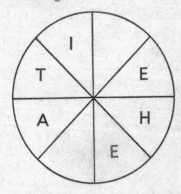

17.   Select the correct figure from the numbered ones.

18. Select the correct figure from the six numbered ones.

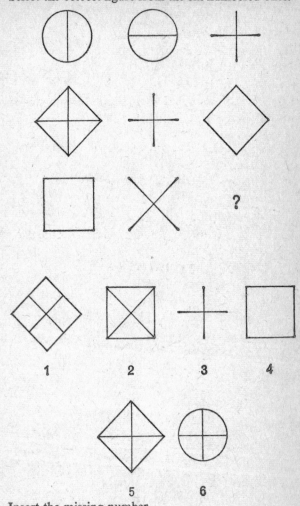

19. Insert the missing number.
    6   11   ?   27

20. Insert the missing number.

12 (56) 16
17 ( ) 21

21. Insert the missing word.

ETHYL (HERO) FROWN
UNTIL (. . . .) ABEAM

22. Insert the word that completes the first word and begins the second.

SP (. . .) OW

23. Find the odd man out.

GABER
YRFRE
NUKKS
THACY

24. Insert the word that means the same as the two words outside the brackets.

LIGHT (. . . . .) COMPETITION

25. Insert the missing letter.

A D G
D H L
H M ?

26. Insert the missing letters.

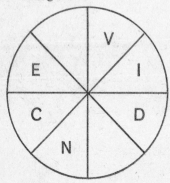

27. Select the correct figure from the six numbered ones.

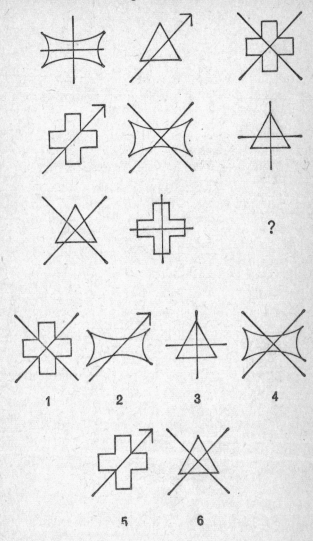

28. Select the correct figure from the numbered ones.

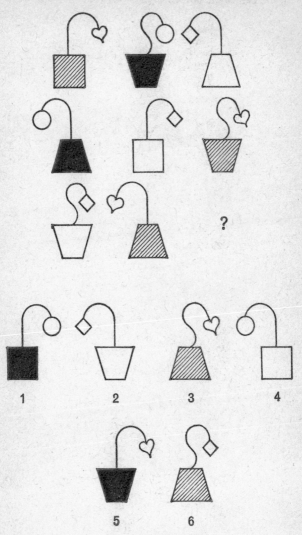

29. Select the correct figure from the six numbered ones.

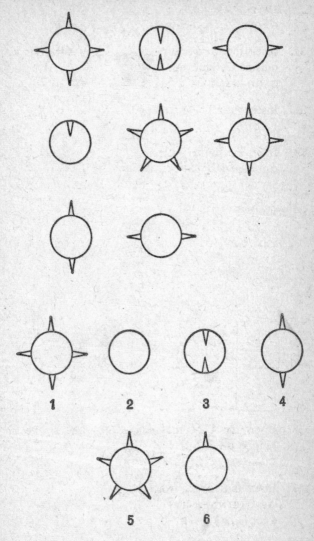

30. Insert the missing word.
SMITH (TIDE) BREAD
GROSS (. . . .) GROWL

31. Insert the word that means the same as the two words outside the brackets.
CARD-GAME (. . . . .) ROD

32. Insert the missing number.
1   8   27   ?

33. Insert the missing word.
CROSS (SORE) RENTS
MAKES (. . . .) INLET

34. Find the odd man out.
LAWL
YESDUTA
OFOR
DIWWON

35. Insert the missing letter and number.

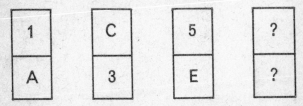

36. Insert the word that means the same as the words outside the brackets.
COMPETITION (. . . .) GROUP

37. Insert the missing word.
GRID (RING) HANG
STIR (. . . .) GAFF

Select the correct figure from the six numbered ones.

1

2

3

4

5

6

39. Select the correct figure from the six numbered ones.

40.   Select the correct figure from the four numbered ones.

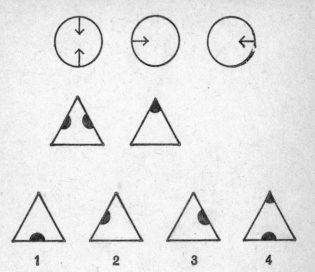

TEST TWO

1. Select the correct figure from the four numbered ones.

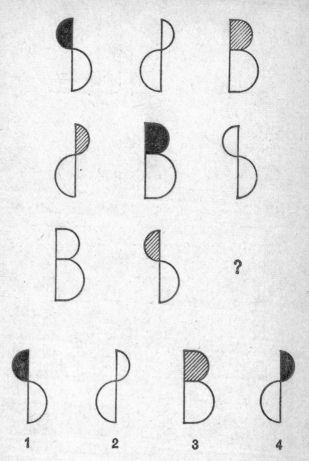

2. Insert the word that completes the first word and begins the second.

INDIVI (....) ISM

3. Insert the missing number.

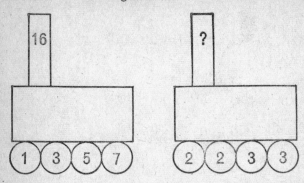

4. Select the correct figure from the six numbered ones.

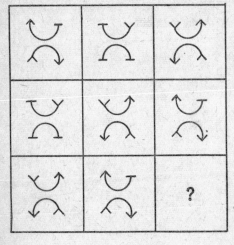

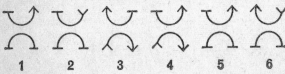

5. Find the odd man out.
NIROY
LEEST
PORPEC
NOBREZ

6. Insert the missing word.
PIECE (CELL) PILLS
GRIPS (. . . .) SWELL

7. Insert the missing number.
143   (56)   255
218   (   )   114

8. Insert the missing number.
6   10   18   34   ?

9. Find the odd man out.
REPLUP
KOYNED
RAEZU
LOITEV

10. Insert the missing number.

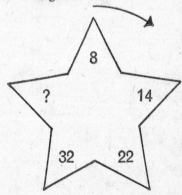

11.   Select the correct figure from the six numbered ones.

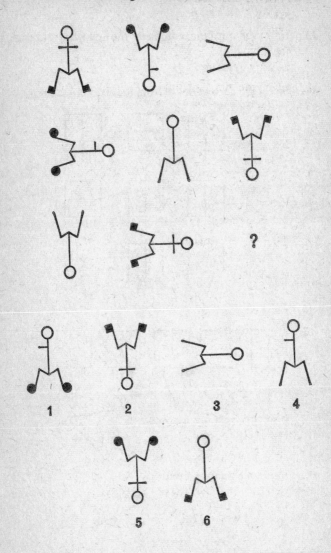

12. Insert the missing letter.

R T P R N P ?

13. Insert the word that completes the first word and begins the second.

THR (. . .) ROUS

14. Select the correct figure from the six numbered ones.

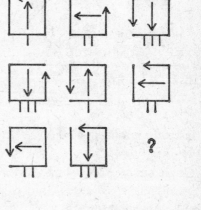

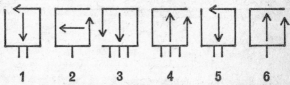

1   2   3   4   5   6

15. Insert the missing number.

148   (110)   368
243   (   )   397

16. Insert the missing number.

18   25   4
16   20   3
 6   15   ?

17. Insert the missing letters.

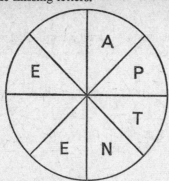

18. Insert the word that completes the first word and begins the second.

AM (. . . .) EL

19. Insert the missing number.

437 (410) 642
541 (   ) 783

20. Insert the missing word.

BOILS (SOOT) STOOP
DIVES (. . . .) AGONY

21. Insert the missing number.

0   3   8   15   ?

22. Find the odd man out.

STUN
PAGRE
MUPL
SNUG

23. Insert the word that means the same as the words outside the brackets.

DRUNK (. . . . .) CLOSE

24. Select the correct figure from the six numbered ones.

25. Insert the missing word.
SING (NINE) SPEND
LONG.(....) CREST

26. Insert the missing number.
1   8   16   25   ?

27. Select the correct figure from the six numbered ones.

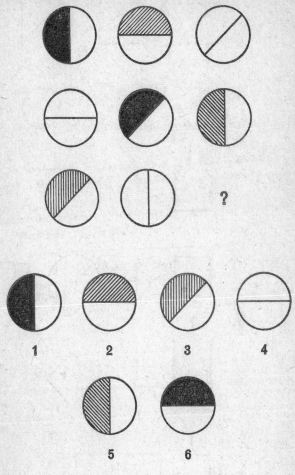

28. Insert the word that means the same as the words outside the brackets.

OPENING (. . . . .) BREAK

29. Insert the missing letter.

A   D   G

D   I   N

I   P   ?

30. Select the correct figure from the six numbered ones.

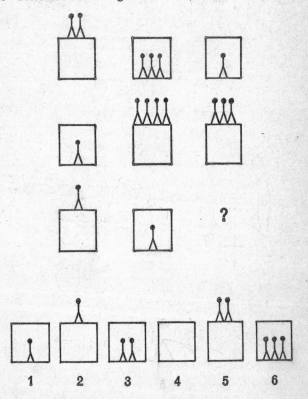

31. Select the correct figure from the six numbered ones.

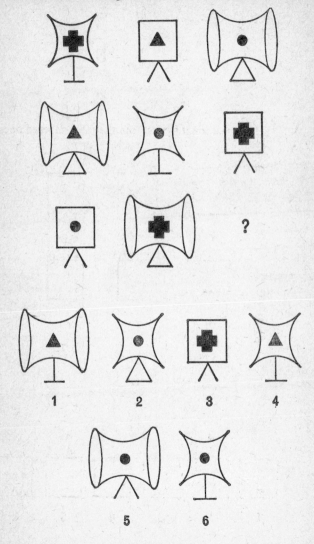

32. Insert the missing letters.

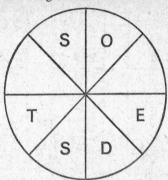

33. Insert the missing word.
GOOSE (SONS) NOOSE
DRINK (. . . .) PLUSH

34. Find the odd man out.
TUEPCIR
NITNIGAP
SHOTCAM
OTHOP

35. Insert the missing letters.

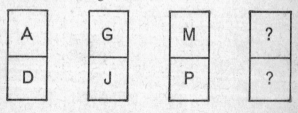

36. Insert the word that means the same as the words outside the brackets.
STAKE (. . . .) MAIL

37.   Select the correct figures from the six numbered ones.

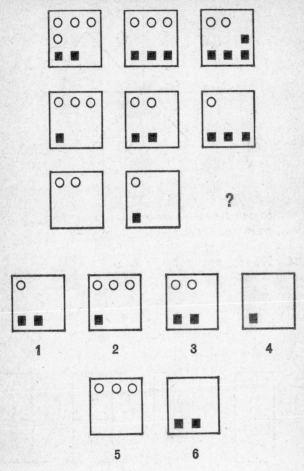

38.   Insert the missing number
   42   (44)   38
   23   (   )   28

39. Select the correct figure from the six numbered ones.

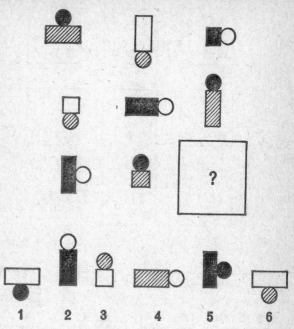

40. Insert the missing word.
STING (SONS) ROOFS
GROAN (....) ALOUD

1. Select the correct figure from the four numbered ones.

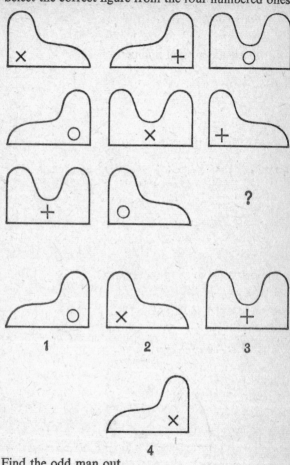

2. Find the odd man out.

KEIP
GEHRNIR
KRASH
ROMFERTOC

3. Insert the word that completes the first word and begins the second.

INDIS (. . . .) R

4. Insert the missing number.

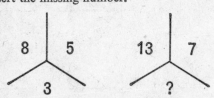

5. Insert the missing word.

GROOM (ROSE) MOUSE

PINCH (. . . .) ONION

6. Insert the missing number.

651 (331) 342

449 ( ) 523

7. Insert the missing number.

8 12 24 60 ?

8. Insert the missing letter.

B F K Q ?

9. Insert the missing number.

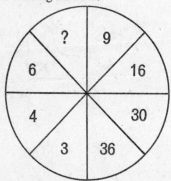

10. Select the correct figure from the six numbered ones.

11. Select the correct figure from the six numbered ones.

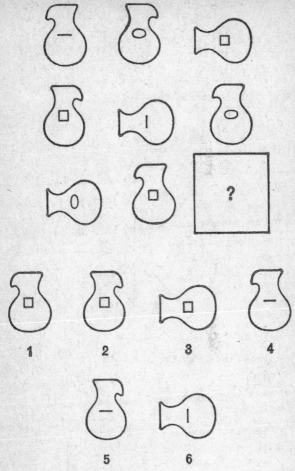

1 2 3 4

5 6

12. Insert the word that completes the first word and begins the second.

UR (...) AL

13. Find the odd man out.

AGENT

BLISS

CHURCH

LOVE

DOLL

14. Insert the missing number.

96 (16) 12

88 ( ) 11

15. Insert the missing letters.

16. Insert the missing number.

2 10 4

3 17 5

3 ? 4

17. Insert the word that completes the first word and begins the second.

SHR (. . .) ALE

18. Insert the missing number.

98 (54) 64

81 ( ) 36

19. Select the correct figure from the six numbered ones.

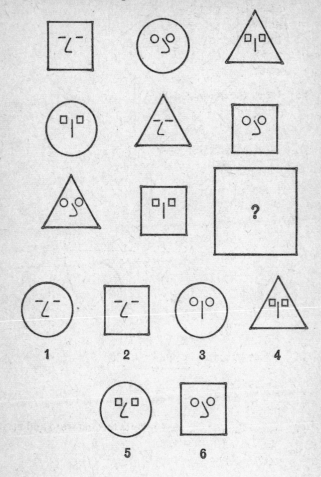

1   **2**   **3**   **4**

5   **6**

20. Insert the missing word.
SLOPE (POOR) GROOM
PLANE (. . . .) SEEMS

21. Select the correct figure from the six numbered ones.

22. Find the odd man out.

LAWHE
SEHO
OBOT
KOCS

23. Select the correct figure from the six numbered ones.

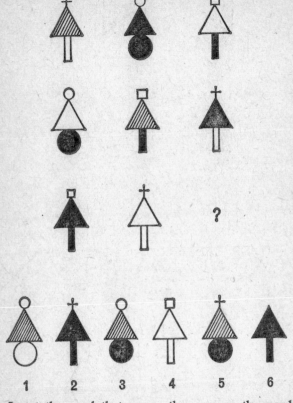

1 2 3 4 5 6

24. Insert the word that means the same as the words outside the brackets.

JOKE (. . .) SILENCE

25. Insert the missing letter.

C F I
D H L
E J ?

26. Select the correct figure from the six numbered ones.

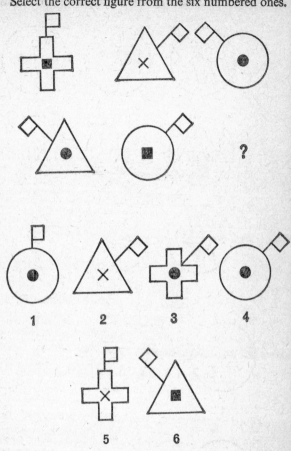

1   **2**   **3**   **4**

5   **6**

27. Insert the missing number.
2 8 5 6 8 ? 11

28. Insert the missing word.
BIRD (DRIP) PILLS
GRIP (. . . .) ELBOW

29. Select the correct figure from the six numbered ones.

30. Insert the missing letters.

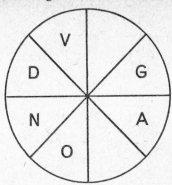

31. Insert the word that means the same as the words outside the brackets.

ARMOUR (....) POST

32. Insert the missing number.

82   97   114   133   ?

33. Insert the missing word.

DRUM (LUMP) GULP

SLIP (....) GODS

34. Find the odd man out.

PEPLA

AANNAB

GENINE

PERRAGITUF

35. Insert the missing number and letter.

2		E		8		?
B		5		H		?

36. Select the correct figure from the six numbered ones.

1   2   3   4   5   6

37. Insert the word that means the same as the words outside the brackets.

EXCAVATION (. . . .) POSSESSION

38. Insert the missing number.

16   (93)   15
14   (   )   12

39. Insert the missing word.

SEND (SEED) FEEL
GAME (. . . .) STAY

40.   Select the correct figure from the six numbered ones.

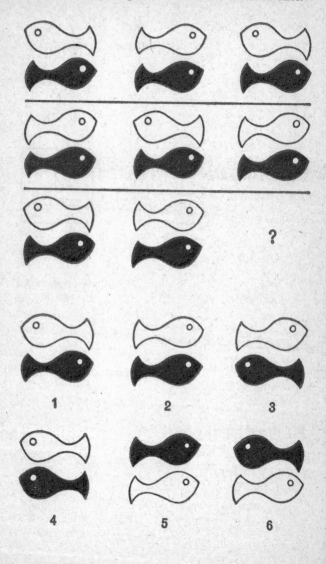

TEST FOUR

1. Select the correct figure from the four numbered ones.

1   2   3   4

2. Insert the word that completes the first word and begins the second.

PYRA (. . .) GET

3. Find the odd man out.

NISOB
NETHELOPE
AZBRE
GIRET

4. Insert the missing word.

QUIPS (PUNT) STERN
QUOTE (. . . .) BEGIN

5. Select the correct figure from the six numbered ones.

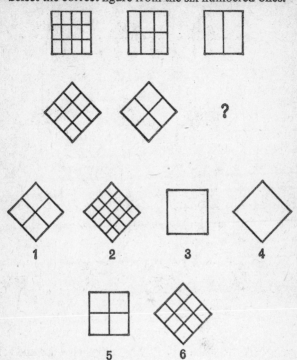

6. Insert the missing number.
112 (190) 17
268 ( ) 107

7. Insert the missing numbers.

5	10	10	17	?
8	7	13	14	?

8. Insert the missing number.

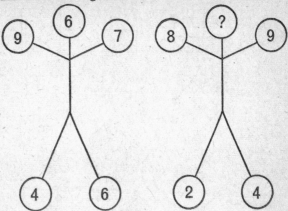

9. Insert the missing number.

6 9 ? 24 36

10. Find the odd man out.

SOEN
REPPA
TALES
NETHCRAMP

11. Insert the missing letters.

12. Select the correct figure from the six numbered ones.

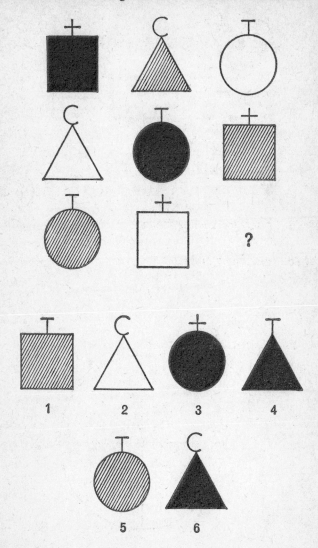

13. Insert the missing letter.

S   P   L   G   ?

14. Select the correct figure from the six numbered ones.

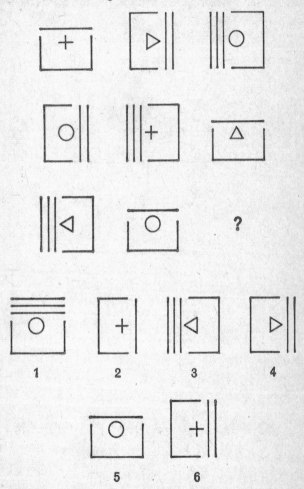

15. Insert the missing number.

16 (96) 12
10 ( ) 15

16. Insert the word that completes the first word and begins the second.

CONTR (. . .) ING

17. Insert the missing number.

4 1 2
2 6 3
3 2 ?

18. Select the correct figure from the six numbered ones.

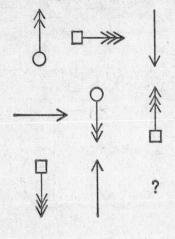

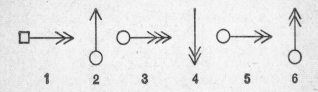

19. Insert the missing number.
2 5 26 ?

20. Select the correct figure from the six numbered ones.

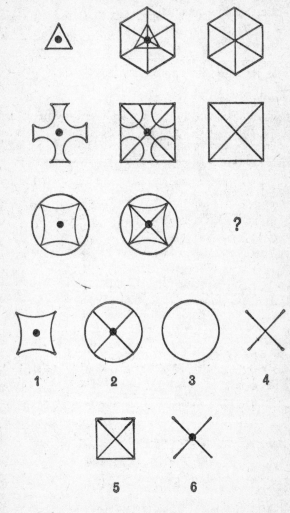

21. Insert the word that completes the first word and begins the second.

DE (....) ROY

22. Insert the missing number.

41 (28) 27
83 ( ) 65

23. Insert the missing word.

SHIRE (HELP) LAMPS
GLOBE (....) NUTTY

24. Select the correct figure from the six numbered ones.

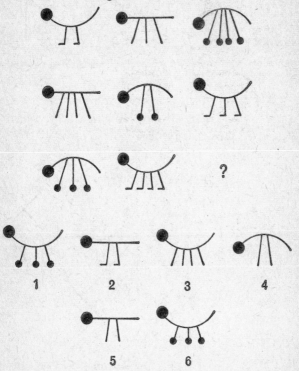

1   2   3   4

5   6

25. Insert the word that means the same as the words outside the brackets.

SAID (. . . . .) BAR

26. Insert the missing letter.

A   D   G
G   K   O
O   T   ?

27. Find the odd man out.

RAHIC
LOTOS
SUMOE
RHENOT

28. Insert the missing word.

GONG (OGLE) ELSE
MARS (. . . .) DIME

29. Insert the missing letters.

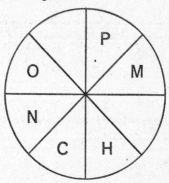

30. Insert the missing number.

65   35   17   ?

31. Select the correct figure from the six numbered ones.

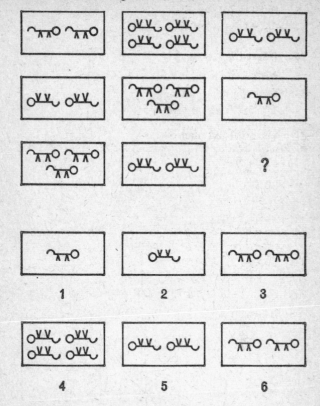

32. Insert the word that means the same as the words outside the brackets.
ROD (....) MAIL

33. Insert the word that means the same as the words outside the brackets.
SMALL (......) MEMORANDUM

34. Find the odd man out.

SEON

HUTOM

HIFS

THAMOCS

NASHD

35. Insert the missing word.

GRACE (READ) DANE

BEARD (....) EGGS

36. Select the correct figure from the six numbered ones.

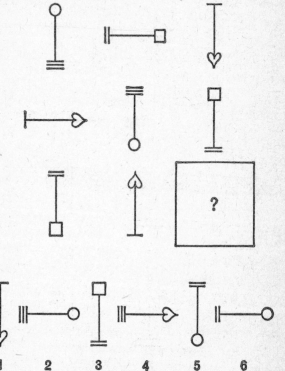

1   2   3   4   5   6

37. Select the correct figure from the six numbered ones.

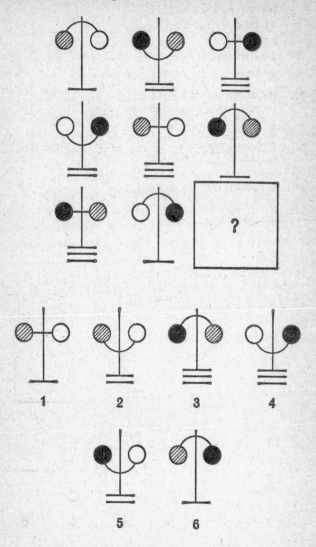

38. Insert the missing word.
GIVE (GONE) FOND
TOUT (....) REST

39. Insert the missing number and letter.

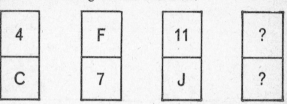

40. Insert the missing number.
8   8   6   2   ?

TEST FIVE

1. Select the correct figure from the four numbered ones.

1   **2**   **3**   **4**

2. Insert the word that completes the first word and begins the second.

WEAT (. . .) MIT

3. Find the odd man out.

PEPMIL
GIDONI
CABLK
THEWI

4. Find the missing number.

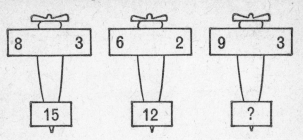

5. Select the correct figure from the six numbered ones.

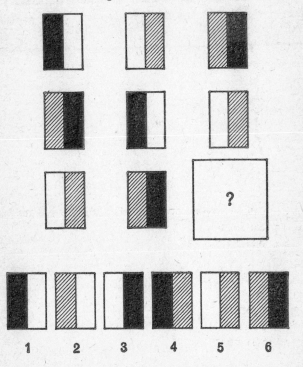

6. Insert the missing number.

5 7 4 6 3 ?

7. Select the correct figure from the six numbered ones.

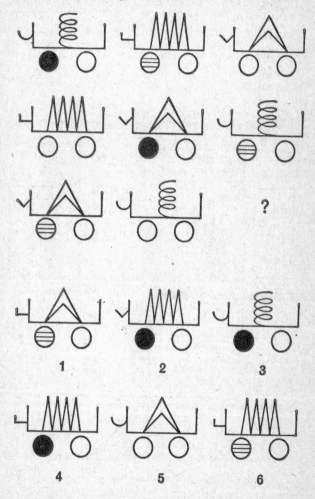

8. Insert the missing word.

PATCH (HALE) SMELL

RANKS (....) RASPS

9. Insert the missing number.

368 (9) 215

444 ( ) 182

10. Find the odd man out.

LEPCIN

LIQUL

HACKL

SOWRM

11. Insert the missing letter.

B E I N ?

12. Insert the missing numbers.

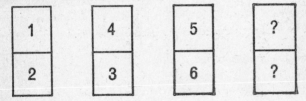

13. Insert the missing letters.

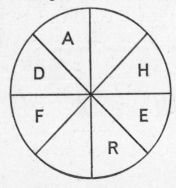

14. Select the correct figure from the six numbered ones.

15. Select the correct figure from the six numbered ones.

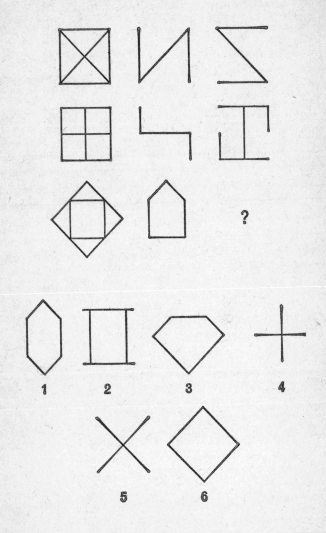

16. Insert the word that completes the first word and begins the second.

BRIG (. . .) IRON

17. Insert the missing number.

836 (316) 112
213 (   ) 420

18. Insert the missing number.

5   8   12
7   12   18
3   4   ?

19. Insert the word that completes the first word and begins the second.

SP (. . .) NA

20. Insert the missing number.

188 (118) 424
214 (   ) 320

21. Insert the missing word.

GRINS (LOIN) ALONE
SWILL (. . . .) ATONE

22. Insert the missing number.

0 7 26 ?

23. Find the odd man out.

MAIR
TIGERTIB
DORHAL
NOCENI

24. Select the correct figure from the six numbered ones.

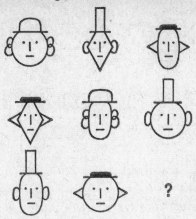

?

1   2   3   4   5   6

25. Insert the word that means the same as the words outside the brackets.

WEIGHT (.....) CORN

26. Insert the missing letter.

```
?  R  T
R  O  E
T  E  A
```

27. Insert the missing number.

71   68   77   50   ?

28. Select the correct figure from the six numbered ones.

29. Insert the missing word.
STING (SITS) ATOMS
BLANK (....) CRAMS

30. Select the correct figure from the six numbered ones.

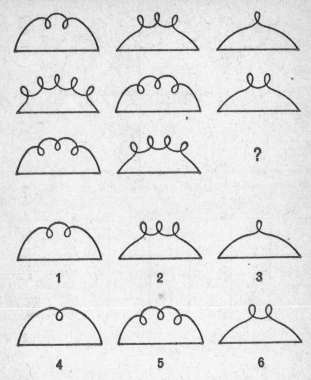

31. Insert the word that means the same as the words outside the brackets.

BOAT (. . . . .) SKILL

32. Find the odd man out.

PATREC

SEUOL

KEDS

RACHI

33. Insert the missing letters.

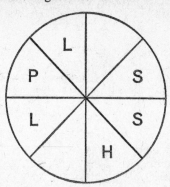

34. Insert the missing letters.

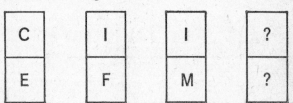

35. Insert the missing word.
GREAT (TOES) ROCKS
PANTS (. . . .) DAVID

36. Insert the word that means the same as the words outside the brackets.
THIN (. . . .) REST

37. Insert the missing word.
DEEP (PEST) FITS
SNAP (?) LIST

38. Select the correct figure from the six numbered ones.

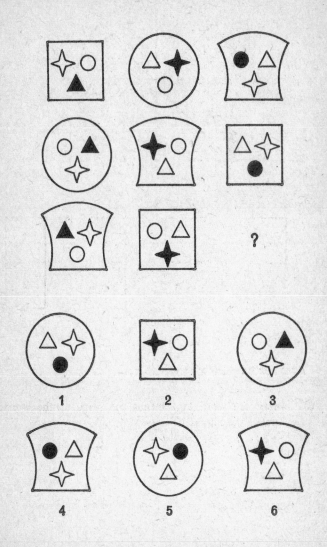

39. Select the correct figure from the six numbered ones.

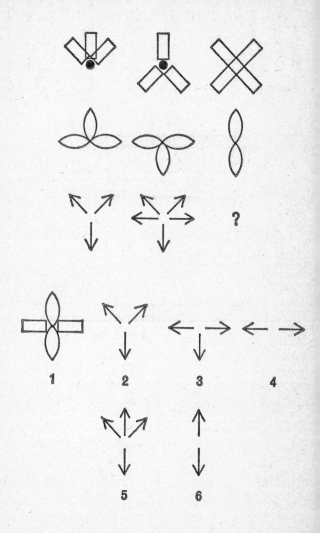

40. Insert the missing numbers.

9	16	7	?
25	8	9	?

1. Insert the word that means the same as the words outside the brackets.

   NEW (. . . . .) TALE

2. Insert the word that completes the first word and begins the second. (Clue: Boy.)

   BAL (. . .) DER

3. Find the odd man out in these anagrams.

   SCHAMOT

   LABLOTOF

   CEKTIRC

   SNINET

4. Find the word-ending which can be prefixed by all of the following.

   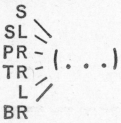

   S
   SL
   PR
   TR
   L
   BR
   (. . .)

5. Insert the word that means the same as the words outside the brackets.

   PUSH (. . . . .) NEWSPAPERS

6. Insert the word that completes the first word and begins the second. (Clue: Finish.)

   TR (. . .) IVE

7. Find the odd man out.

   TIRANAS

   TINLOM

   RYBOCS

   RYLESEP

8. Insert the word that can precede the three words at the right.

$$(\ . \ . \ . \ . \ . \ )\begin{cases} \text{BIRD} \\ \text{BALL} \\ \text{LEG} \end{cases}$$

9. Insert the word that means the same as the words outside the brackets.

FRIEND (. . . .) JOIN

10. Insert the word that completes the first word and begins the second.

EX (. . . .) ACLE

11. Find the odd man out.

STOP

DRIOA

PENOH

DREAGN

12. Insert the word that can precede the three words at the right.

$$(\ . \ . \ . \ . \ )\begin{cases} \text{TREE} \\ \text{HORN} \\ \text{LACE} \end{cases}$$

13. Insert the word that completes the first word and begins the second.

SP (. .) CH

14. Insert the word that means the same as the words outside the brackets.

CUT (. . . .) OPENING

15. Find the odd man out.

TRACROS

TEADS

LEPAPS

RESHICER

BABECAGS

16. Find the word which can be prefixed by all the following.

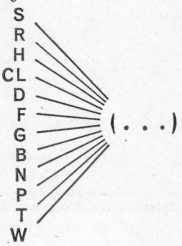

17. Insert the word that completes the first word and begins the second.

ST (...) PLE

18. Find the odd man out.

HARCI

NOPEY

PYPOP

CUTREBPUT

LIPUT

19. Find the word which can be prefixed by all the following.

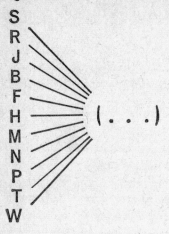

20. Insert the word that means the same as the words outside the brackets.

PUNISH (. . . .) NICE

21. Insert the word that completes the first word and begins the second.

APR (. .) ION

22. Find the odd man out.

REETIRR

STALANIA

XEBOR

LUNTAW

23. Insert the word that means the same as the words outside the brackets.

FLAME (. . . .) SHOOT

24. Find the word-ending which can be prefixed by all the following.

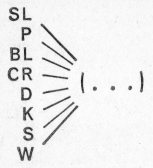

SL
P
BL
CR
D
K
S
W

(. . .)

25. Insert the word that completes the first word and begins the second.

ST (. . . .) ER

26. Find the odd man out.

RUYERS

SEEXS

NOLLWARC

AROLFID

27. Insert the word which means the same as the words outside the brackets.

CROWD (. . . . .) NEWSPAPERS

28. Insert the word that completes the first word and begins the second.

A (. . . .) Y

29. Find the odd man out.

OCIRA

OKOTI

OOTRONT

REBLAGED

30. Find the word-ending which can be prefixed by all the following.

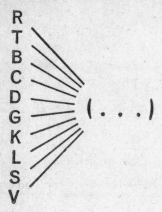

R
T
B
C
D
G
K
L
S
V

(. . .)

31. Find the word-ending which can be prefixed by all of the following:

FL
TH
R
K
P
S
W
ST

(. . .)

32. Insert the word that means the same as the words outside the brackets.

SHAPE (. . . .) CLASS

33. Insert the word that completes the first word and begins the second.

HAM (. . . . . .) ENT

34. Find the odd man out.

LEEGA

WARPSOR

RALK

LAHEW

35. Find the word-ending which can be prefixed by all of the following:

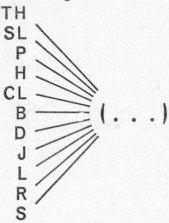

TH
SL
P
H
CL
B
D
J
L
R
S

(. . .)

36. Insert the word that completes the first word and begins the second. (Clue: Pitch.)

S (. . .) GET

37. Find the odd man out.

KINSECD

SLEWL

NIENIEST

FEDEO

TISWF

38. Insert the word that means the same as the words outside the brackets.

ACCOUNT (....) BEAK

39. Find the word-ending which can be prefixed by all of the following:

D
H
L
M   (. . .)
P
T

40. Insert the word that means the same as the words outside the brackets.

NOTCH (....) CATCH

41. Insert the word that completes the first word and begins the second.

DEC (....) AGE

42. Find the odd man out.
LIONSTEVIE
OIQSMTOU
TANG
EMITTER

43. Insert the word that means the same as the words outside the brackets.

NEW (.....) IMPUDENT

44. Insert the word that completes the first word and begins the second.

DE (....) ER

45. Find the word-ending which can be prefixed by all of the following:

46. Find the odd man out.

SHROPAMEE

TOGA

RHOSE

VABERE

47. Find the word-ending which can be prefixed by all of the following:

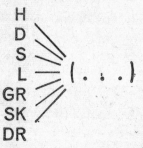

48. Insert the word that completes the first word and begins the second.

ENC (....) LES

49. Find the word which can be prefixed by all of the
    following letters:

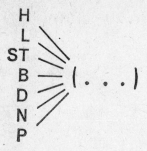

50. Find the odd man out.
    TORREBH
    STERIS
    LINOVI
    NUTA
    HOTMER

NUMERICAL ABILITY

1. Insert the missing number.
18 20 24 32 ?

2. Insert the missing number.

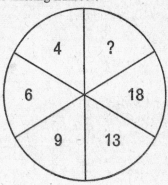

3. Insert the missing number.
212 179 146 113 ?

4. Insert the missing number.

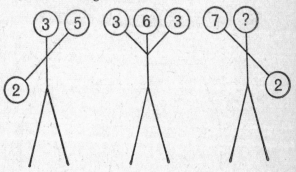

5. Insert the missing number.
6 8 10 11 14 14 ?

6. Insert the missing number.
   17 (112) 39
   28 (   ) 49

7. Insert the missing number.
   3 9 3
   5 7 1
   7 1 ?

8. Insert the missing number.
   7 13 24 45 ?

9. Insert the missing number.
   234 (333) 567
   345 (   ) 678

10. Insert the missing number.
   4 5 7 11 19 ?

11. Insert the missing number.

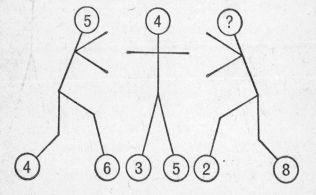

12. Insert the missing number.
6   7   9   13   21   ?

13. Insert the missing number.
4   8   6
6   2   4
8   6   ?

14. Insert the missing number.
64   48   40   36   34   ?

15. Insert the missing number.

2	6
54	18

?	9
81	27

16. Insert the missing number.
718   (26)   582
474   (   )   226

17. Insert the missing number.
15   13   12   11   9   9   ?

18. Insert the missing number.
9   4   1
6   6   2
1   9   ?

19. Insert the missing number.
11   12   14   ?   26   42

20. Insert the missing number.

```
8  5  2
4  2  0
9  6  ?
```

21. Insert the missing number.

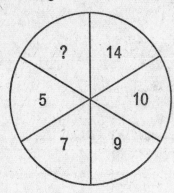

22. Insert the missing number.

```
341  (250)  466
282  (   )  398
```

23. Insert the missing number.

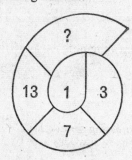

24. Insert the missing number.
12 (336) 14
15 (   ) 16

25. Insert the missing number.
4 7 6
8 4 8
6 5 ?

26. Insert the missing number.
7 14 10 12 14 9 ?

27. Insert the missing number.

8 5   2 1   11 6   3 5

28. Insert the missing number.
17 (102) 12
14 (   ) 11

29. Insert the missing number.
172 84 40 18 ?

30. Insert the missing number.
1 5 13 29 ?

31. Insert the missing number.

32. Insert the missing number.

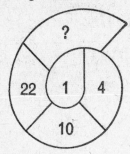

33. Insert the missing number.
0   3   8   15   ?

34. Insert the missing number.
1   3   2   ?   3   7

35. Insert the missing number.
447 (366) 264
262 (   ) 521

36. Insert the missing number.

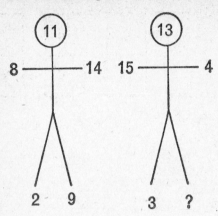

37. Insert the missing number.
4   7   9   11   14   15   19   ?

38. Insert the missing number.

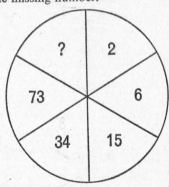

39. Insert the missing number.
3   7   16
6   13   28
9   19   ?

40. Insert the missing numbers.

2	5	9	14	?
4	8	13	19	?

41. Insert the missing number.

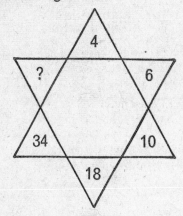

42. Insert the missing number.

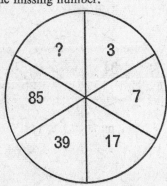

43. Insert the missing number.

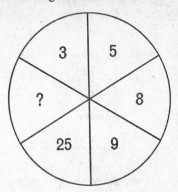

44. Insert the missing number.
643   (111)   421
269   (   )   491

45. Insert the missing number.
857   969   745   1193   ?

46. Insert the missing number.

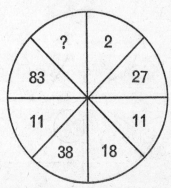

47. Insert the missing numbers.
  9 (45) 81
  8 (36) 64
  10 (?) ?

48. Insert the missing number.
  7 19 37 61 ?

49. Insert the missing number.
  5 41 149 329 ?

50. Insert the missing number.

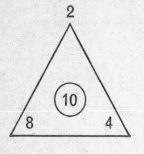

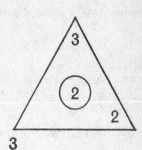

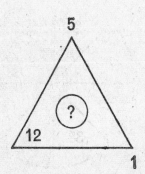

VISUO-SPATIAL ABILITY

1. Find the odd man out.

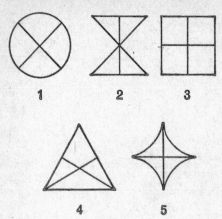

2. Find the odd man out.

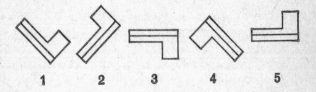

3. Find the odd man out.

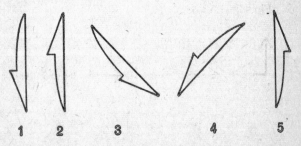

4. Find the odd man out.

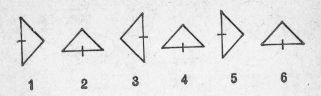

5. Find the odd man out.

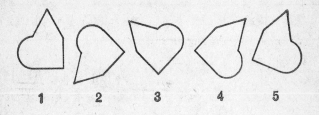

6. Find the odd man out.

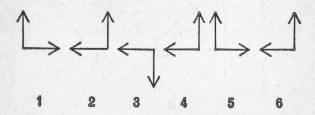

7. Find the odd man out.

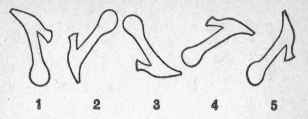

1   **2**   **3**   **4**   **5**

8. Insert the missing figure.

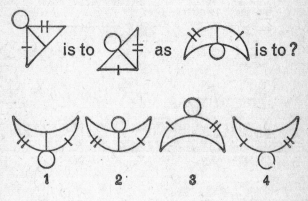

1   **2**   **3**   **4**

9. Find the odd man out.

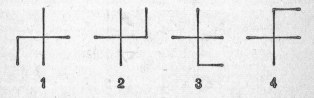

1   **2**   **3**   **4**

10.   Find the odd man out.

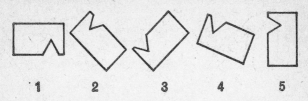

11.   Find the odd man out.

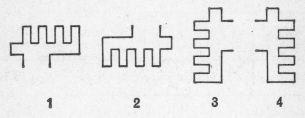

12.   Find the odd man out.

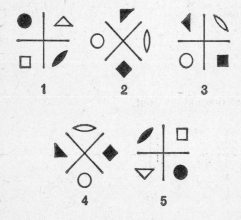

13. Find the odd man out.

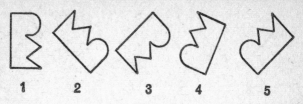

14. Find the odd man out.

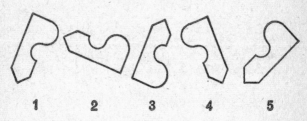

15. Find the odd man out.

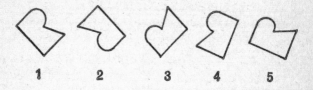

16. Find the odd man out.

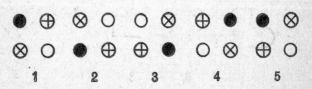

17. Find the odd man out.

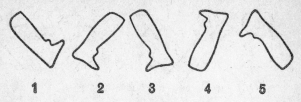

18. Find the odd man out.

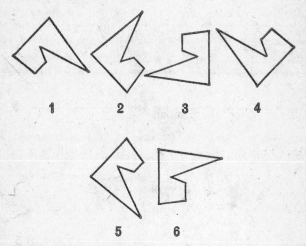

19. Find the odd man out.

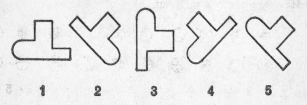

20. Find the odd man out.

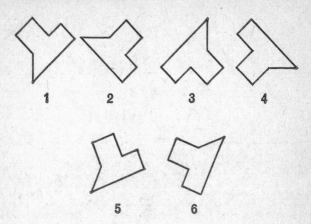

21. Find the odd man out.

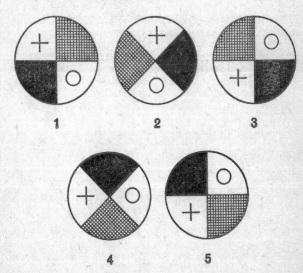

22. Find the odd man out.

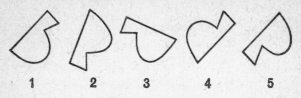

1   2   3   4   5

23. Find the odd man out.

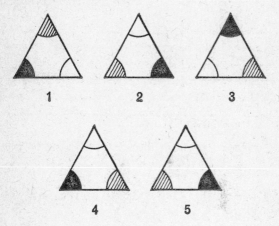

1   2   3

4   5

24. Find the odd man out.

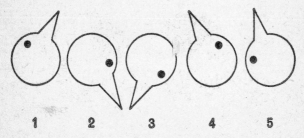

1   2   3   4   5

25. Find the odd man out.

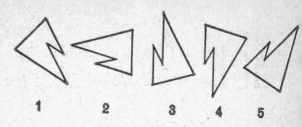

26. Find the odd man out.

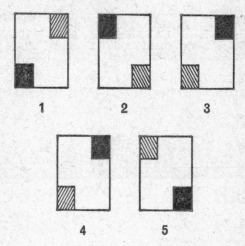

27. Find the odd man out.

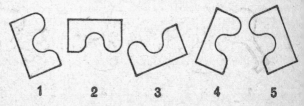

28. Insert the missing figure.

is to ... as ... is to ?

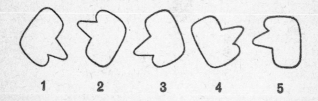

1   2   3   4

29. Find the odd man out.

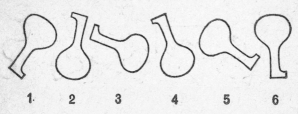

1   2   3   4   5

30. Find the odd man out.

1.   2   3   4   5   6

31. Insert the missing figure.

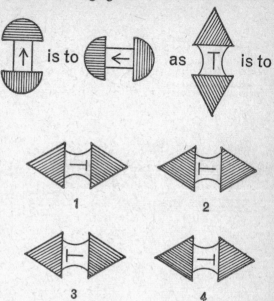

32. Find the odd man out.

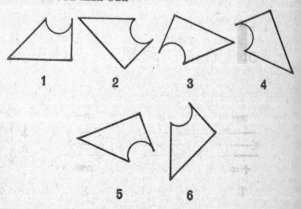

33. Find the two odd men out.

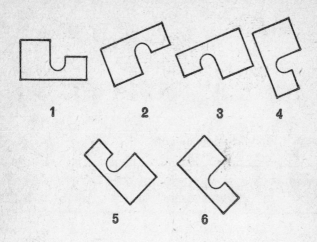

1   2   3   4

5   6

34. Insert the missing figure.

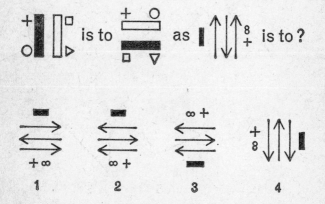

1   2   3   4

35. Find the two odd men out.

36. Find the odd man out.

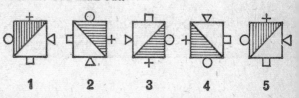

37. Insert the missing figure.

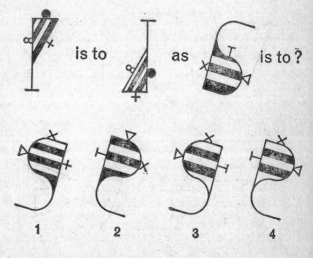

38. Insert the missing figure.

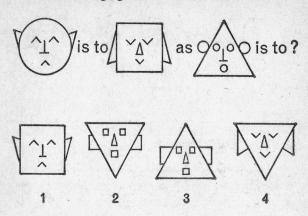

39. Find the two odd men out.

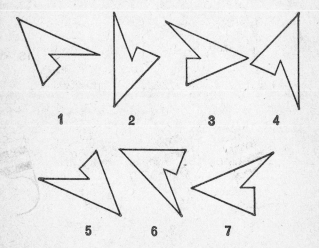

40. Find the three odd men out.

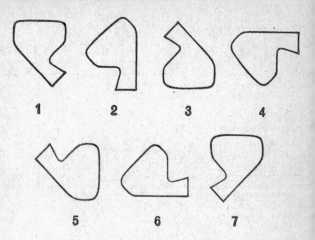

41. Find the three odd men out.

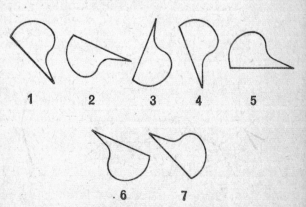

42. Find the two odd men out.

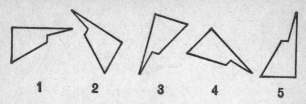

43. Find the odd man out.

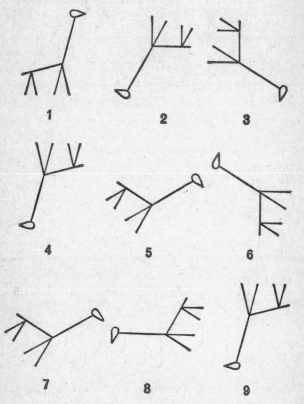

44. Insert the missing figure.

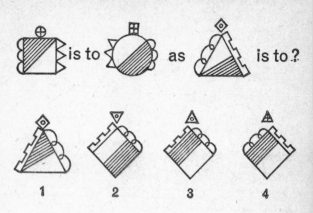

45. Find the three odd men out.

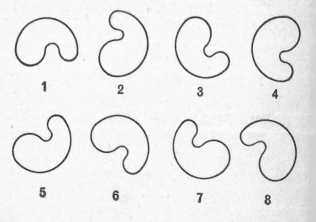

46. Find the odd man out.

Turn to next page for question 47.

47. Find the three odd men out.

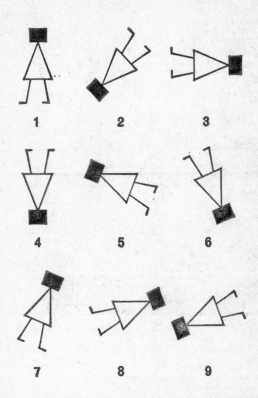

48. Find the three odd men out.

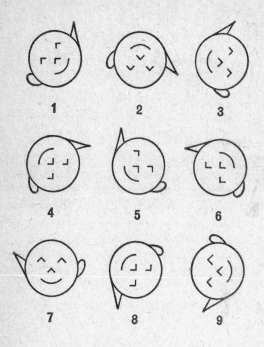

Turn to next page for question 49.

49. Find the three odd men out.

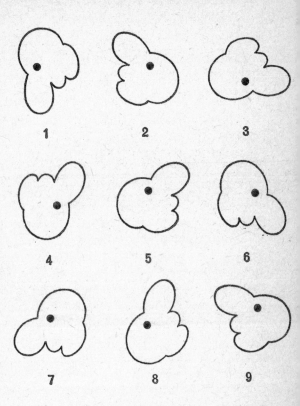

50.   Find the odd man out.

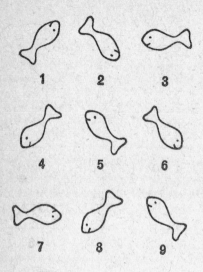

LIMBERING UP FOR
INTELLECTUAL GIANTS I

The following two tests are not I.Q. tests and cannot be scored. They are very difficult, and if you get through one of them in an evening, getting even half of the answers right, you are unlikely to have an I.Q. below that of the average college student. If you get more than that right you are really doing well. If you have an average I.Q. you may not get any right, or only one or two. These are very rough guides; it is impossible that tests at this difficulty level could be more precise.

1. Insert the missing numbers.

3	7	13	21	?
5	20	51	104	?

2. UNUSUAL is to UNPREPOSSESSING
as UNDULATING is to ?
DUBIOUS PREPONDERANCE INSOLUBLE
CONTINUOUS ROUNDABOUT

3. Insert the missing number.
118 199 226 235 ?

4. If GIBE — FADE = 81, then
DICE — CEDE = ?

5. REPUBLICAN = 108
DEMOCRAT = ?

6. LOUSE is to SCALP
as HOUND is to ?
PIXIE ACTOR GUSTO HOURI SHAFT

7. Insert the missing number.
7 10 ? 94 463

8. GENERATION = 95
TELEVISION = ?

9. Insert the missing letter.
B   C   E   J   ?

10. HOLY is to SLOB
as LOW is to ?
ONE   OLD   GLOW   BOW   SOW

11. Insert the missing number.
0   2   8   18   ?

12. Insert the missing number, standing up:
$8\frac{2}{3}$ $11\frac{3}{4}$? $12\frac{2}{3}$

13. Continue the series:
1   1   2   3   5   8   13   21   ?
There are two ways of finding the answer, an easy one
and a difficult one. See if you can find both.

14. Insert the missing number.
ARID = 80
DEAR = 89
RAID = 63
READ = ?

15. Insert the missing number.
2   20   42   68   ?

16. Insert the missing number.
REWARDED   = 80
COORDINATE   = 75
OPINIONATED   = ?

17. Find the odd man out.
SUPERCILIOUSNESS CONSCIOUSLY INIMITABLE
EXTERMINATORY SEPARATED

18. Insert the missing number.

CAGE	BEG	BIDE
+ FAD	—HID	—FADE
= 2227	= 563	= ?200

19. BAROMETER is to GASOMETER as PUGILISM is to ?
LIGHTNING PROTECTIONISM CRUISING
BIMETALLISM

20. Insert the 4 missing numbers.
(172 4 327 628) (67 4 19)
(4) (147 84 403 403 147 28) (? ? ? ?)

LIMBERING UP FOR
INTELLECTUAL GIANTS II

1. Insert the missing number.
   $3\frac{1}{2}$ 4 7 14 49 ?

2. If CARUSO = 84 and GIGLI = 56,
   how much is CROSBY worth?

3. Insert the missing number.
   8 10 16 34 ?

4. DRIVER = 7
   PEDESTRIAN = 11
   ACCIDENT = ?

5. EVE — ADAM = JOAN – ?
   BILL DON JOHN MIKE ART

6. PASTICHE = PESTILENCE = ?
   LASCIVIOUS PISTACHIO SENTIMENT
   PUMPERNICKEL

7. Insert the missing letter.
   E N S J ?

8. REMBRANDT = 83
   CEZANNE = 48
   CONSTABLE = ?

9. Find the odd man out.
   JOT FED DIN GUT WOG

10. If a girl without a boy is poor, and if she is worth 20, what is he worth?

11. Insert the missing number.
—1 —1 1 11 49 ?

12. Find the odd man out.
CRANK MESS HARLOT FARTHER BABYLON

13. POMEGRANATES — PIEBALD
= PILLIWINKLE — ?
PISTACHIO PASTICHE PETROL PESTILENCE

14. Insert the missing number.
3 24 4
5 120 100
1 0 ?

15. Find the odd man out.
SIR MAN FIG TON HOG

16. ZN + XT = TZ
and ZV + ZR = ZJR
what is Z + Z?

17. ELECTRICITY — GAS = 100
JACK — JILL = ?

18. Insert the missing number.
7 49 441 ?

19. Insert the first number in the series. (It is not 2!)
? 3 4 6 8 12

20. How many children has Albert?

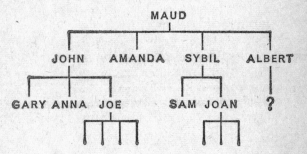

ANSWERS AND EXPLANATIONS

1. 4.

2. ICE.

3. MUDBATH. (All the others are kitchen utensils: bowl, spoon, plate.)

4. 11. (Subtracting the number on the door from the sum of the numbers in the windows gives the number on the roof.)

5. ROSE. (The first letter of the word in brackets is the second letter of the first word, the second is the fourth letter of the first word, the third is the fifth letter of the second word, the fourth is the third letter of the second word.)

6. 25. (Add the six digits outside the brackets together.)

7. 3. (Each number is obtained by adding 2 to the previous one, and then dividing by 2; $4 + 2 = 6$; 6 divided by $2 = 3$.)

8. MACARONI. (All the others are furniture: table, chair, carpet.)

9. 6. (Circle, triangle, and square may be an outer or an inner figure; the inner figure may be black, white, or shaded. Each feature occurs only once in each row and column.)

10. 5. (There are three figures, depending on the line in the centre of the rectangle and three small figures inside: cross, lozenge, and spot; these appear in two places in each rectangle.)

11. F. (Skip 2 and 3 steps back in the alphabet alternately.)

12. INK.

13. 54. (The numbers on the left half of the circle are 3 times the opposite numbers of the right half.)

14. 11. (Take half the first number in each row, add twice the second number, and you get the third.)

15. 27. (The number in the brackets is the difference between the numbers outside the brackets.)

16. s and t. (The word reads HESITATE in an anti-clockwise direction.)

17. 2. (The circle may have no lines, or vertical or horizontal lines, and the small circles outside may be in one of three positions. They also have different shading.)

18. 2. (The figure in the third column is made up of the lines from the figures in the first two columns which are not in common to both.)

19. 18. (Square numbers 2, 3, 4, 5 respectively, adding 2 each time.)

20. 76. (Add the numbers outside the bracket and double the sum.)

21. TUBE. (The first letter of the word in the bracket is the third letter of the first word, the second is the first letter of the first word, the third is the second letter of the second word, the fourth is the third letter of the second word.)

22. END.

23. SKUNK. (All the others are boats: barge, ferry, yacht.)

24. MATCH.

25. R. (Skip 2, 3, and 4 letters respectively in the three rows.)

26. E and E. (The word reads EVIDENCE in a clockwise direction.)

27. 2. (There are three types of main figure on which are a cross, an arrow, or an X.)

28. 1. (There are three kinds of vase, each black, white, or shaded; three kinds of stem; and three kinds of flower. Each of these occurs only once in each row and column.)

29. 1. (Spikes outside the circle count +1; inside they count −1. 2 + 2 = 4.)

30. SOLO. (The first letter of the word in brackets is the fourth letter of the first word, the second is the third letter of the first word, the third is the fifth letter of the second word, the fourth is the third letter of the second word.)

31. POKER.

32. 64. (Cube numbers 1, 2, 3, 4 respectively.)

33. SKIN. (The first letter of the word in brackets is the fifth letter of the first word, the second is the third letter of the first word, the third is the first letter of the second word, the fourth is the second letter of the second word.)

34. TUESDAY. (Wall, roof, and window are parts of a house.)

35.

G
7

(Letters ascend by two alternately from numerator to denominator and similarly the numbers (which correspond to the letters in the alphabet).)

36. RACE.

37. TIFF. (The first letter of the word in the brackets is the second letter of the first word, the second is the third letter of the first word, the third is the third letter of the second word, the fourth is the fourth letter of the second word.)

38. 1. (In each row and column, there are three different shapes of ball, three shapes of head, three types of boot, and three positions of the arms; those not occurring in the two drawings in the last row and column must appear in the missing figure.)

39. 6. (There are three types of skirt, three positions of arms, and three kinds of feet.)

40. 1. (The second and third figures in each row contain inside one each of the two small inside figures of the first drawing, rotated through 90 degrees.)

Test Two

1. 4. (There are three figures, and three kinds of shading.)

2. DUAL.

3. 10. (The sum of the numbers in the wheels of the train gives the number in the funnel.)

4. 2. (There are three endings for the curved lines: arrow-end, arrow-head, and straight line. In each of the four positions, each of these endings occurs only once in each row and column.)

5. IRONY. (All the others are metals: steel, copper, bronze.)

6. PILE. (The first letter of the word in brackets is the fourth letter of the first word, the second is the third letter of the first word, the third is the fourth letter of the second word, the fourth is the third letter of the second word.)

7. 52. (Take the difference between the two numbers outside the brackets; then divide by 2. 218 — 114 = 104; 104 ÷ 2 = 52.)

8. 66. (Each number is twice the previous one, minus 2.)

9. DONKEY. (All the others are colours: purple, azure, violet.)

10. 44. (Moving in a clockwise direction starting at the top: add 6 to the first number to get the second, then increase the previous additional number by 2 each time. Thus 8 + 6 = 14; 14 + 8 = 22; 22 + 10 = 32; 32 + 12 = 44.)

11. 1. (There are three types of arms: nought, one, or two; three types of shoe: nought, square, or round; and three different positions.)

12. L. (Move 2 forward and 4 back alternately.)

13. ONE.

14. 6. (There are three positions for the arrow inside the square and three positions for the arrow on the outside of the square; there are 1, 2, or 3 supports.)

15. 77. (Subtract the left-hand number from the right-hand number and divide by two.)

16. 3. (Subtract second row from first row and multiply by three to get third row.)

17. V and M. (The word reads PAVEMENT, in an anti-clockwise direction.)

18. BUSH.

19. 484. (Multiply the difference between the outer numbers by two.)

20. SING. (The first letter of the word in the brackets is the fifth letter of the first word, the second is the second letter of the first word, the third is the fourth letter of the second word, the fourth is the second letter of the second word.)

21. 24. (Square the numbers 1 to 5 and subtract one each time.)

22. GUNS. (All the others are fruit: nuts, grape, plum.)

23. TIGHT.

24. 5. (The figure in the third column is made up of the lines from the figures in the first two columns which are not common to both.)

25. NOSE. (The first letter of the word in brackets is the third letter of the first word, the second is the second letter of the first word, the third is the fourth letter of the second word, the fourth is the third letter of the second word.)

26. 35. (Add 7, 8, 9, 10 respectively to each number to get the next number.)

27. 6. (The circles can be halved with vertical, horizontal, or diagonal lines, and are either shaded, black, or white.)

28. CRACK.

29. w. (To get from the letters in column 2 to those in column 3, skip as many letters in the alphabet as you have to skip to get from column 1 to column 2. Thus I to P skips 6 letters, and 6 skipped from P gives you W.)

30. 4. (Men outside the square count +1, inside —1. 1 — 1 = 0.)

31. 4. (There are three main figures, three small figures inside the main ones, and three supports.)

32. P and I. (The word reads DEPOSITS in an anti-clockwise direction.)

33. NIPS. (The first letter of the word in the bracket is the fourth letter of the first word, the second is the third letter of the first word, the third is the first letter of the second word, the fourth is the fourth letter of the second word.)

34. STOMACH. (Picture, painting, and photo are all reproductions of something.)

35.

S
V

(The letters go up by three each time, first from numerator to denominator, then to the next numerator, then denominator etc.)

36. POST.

37. 6. (Circles decrease in number going from left to right, squares increase.)

38. 55. (Multiply the difference between the numbers outside the brackets by 11.)

39. 6. (There are three kinds of rectangle, and three positions for the circle; in addition, circle and rectangle can be either white, black, or shaded. None of these four characteristics is repeated in any row or column.)

40. GLAD. (The first letter of the word in the brackets is the first letter of the first word, the second is the second letter of the second word, the third is the fourth letter of the first word, the fourth is the fifth letter of the second word.)

Test Three

1. 4. (There are three main figures, and within each a cross, a circle, or a plus sign.)

2. COMFORTER. (All the others are fish: pike, herring, shark.)

3. POSE.

4. 6. (The sum of the numbers in the right and bottom sectors equal that in the left-hand section.)

5. ICON. (The first letter of the word in brackets is the second letter of the first word, the second is the fourth letter of the first word, the third is the fourth letter of the second word, the fourth is the fifth letter of the second word.)

6. 324. (Add the numbers outside the brackets and divide by 3.)

7. 168. (Multiply each number by 3 and take away 12.)

8. X. (The letters go up by 4, 5, 6, 7 steps.)

9. 6. (Divide the numbers on the right by 3, 4, 5, and 6 respectively to get the numbers in the opposite diagonal.)

10. 5. (There are three kinds of shading, on either side of the figure; each occurs only once in each row and column.)

11. 5. (Each row has one of the three figures and one of the three insets.)

12. BAN.

13. LOVE. (The words all begin with ascending letters of the alphabet, A, B, C, D, but LOVE does not fit into this series.)

14. 16. (Divide the left-hand side by the right-hand side and multiply by two.)

15. D and R. (the word reads SOLDIERS in a clockwise direction.)

16. 14. (Multiply the first and third columns and add two to get the second column.)

17. IMP.

18. 39. (Add the numbers outside the brackets and divide by 3 to get the number inside the brackets.)

19. 1. (There are three shapes, three noses, three types of eyes.)

20. NAME. (The first letter of the word in brackets is the fourth letter of the first word, the second is the third letter of the first word, the third is the fourth letter of the second word, the fourth is the second letter of the second word.)

21. 3. (The third column contains lines which are in common to columns one and two.)

22. WHALE. (All the others are footwear: shoe, boot, sock.)

23. 3. (Triangles can be white, black, or shaded, and there are three types of base and of top.)

24. GAG.

25. O. (The letters go up by 3, 4, 5 respectively along the rows, and by 1, 2, 3 respectively in columns.)

26. 5. (There are three main figures, three small ones inside the main ones, and three positions of the flag.)

27. 4. (There are two series. One going up by 3 each time, alternately with the other which goes down by 2 each time.)

28. PILE. (The first letter of the word in brackets is the fourth letter of the first word, the second is the third letter of the first word, the third is the second letter of the second word, the fourth is the first letter of the second word.)

29. 3. (Men count +1, women —1; 2 — 2 = 0.)

30. A and B. (The word reads VAGABOND in a clockwise direction.)

31. MAIL.

32. 154. (Add numbers 15, 17, 19, 21 respectively.)

33. DIPS. (The first letter of the word in brackets is the third letter of the second word, the second is the third letter of the first word, the third is the fourth letter of the first word, the fourth is the fourth letter of the second word.)

34. Engine. (Apple, banana, and grapefruit are fruits.)

35.

K
11

(The letters and numbers respectively go up by three places, alternating from numerator to denominator.)

36. 1. (There are three sizes of triangle, three kinds of shading, three different positions for the circle, and either one, two, or three legs. Each of these is only found once in each row or column.)

37. MINE.

38. 78. (Add the numbers outside the brackets and multiply by 3 to get the number inside the brackets.)

39. GATE. (The first letter of the word in brackets is the first letter of the first word, the second is the third letter of the second word, the third is the second letter of the second word, the fourth is the fourth letter of the first word.)

40. 1. (All black fish turn to the right, white fish alternate right and left.)

Test Four

1. 1. (There are two, three, or four legs, and a pointed, rectangular, or round top.)

2. MID.

3. TELEPHONE. (All the others are animals: bison, zebra, tiger.)

4. TUNE. (The first letter of the word in brackets is the fourth letter of the first word, the second is the second letter of the first word, the third is the fifth letter of the second word, the fourth is the second letter of the second word.)

5. 4. (Lines diminish by one, going from left to right.)

6. 322. (Twice the difference between the numbers outside the brackets gives the number in the brackets.)

7.

19
22

(There are two series alternating from numerator to denominator each going up by 2, 3, 4, and 5.)

8. 11. (Subtract the sum of the feet from the sum of the hands to get the number in the head.)

9. 15. (Add 3, then 6, then 9, and finally 12.)

10. NOSE. (All the others are writing materials: paper, slate, parchment.)

11. U and D. (The word reads THURSDAY in an anti-clockwise direction.)

12. 6. (There are three main figures, three types of shading, and three different figures on the top.)

13. A. (The letters go back by 2, 3, 4, 5.)

14. 6. (The opening can be up, left, or right; inside can be a cross, a triangle, or a circle; over it one, two, or three lines.)

15. 75. (Multiply the left- and right-hand numbers and divide by two.)

16. ACT.

17. 4. (Each column adds up to 9.)

18. 5. (The arrow can point in one of three directions and it can have 1, 2, or 3 tips. There are also 3 different ends.)

19. 677. (Square each number and add 1 to get the next term.)

20. 4. (The third figure consists of the lines of the second figure minus those of the first.)

21. VICE.

22. 36. (Subtract the right-hand number from the left-hand one and then double it.)

23. LENT. (The first letter of the word in the bracket is the second letter of the first word, the second is the fifth letter of the first word, the third is the first letter of the second word, the fourth is the fourth letter of the second word.)

24. 5. (Animals differ by body shape, number of legs, and type of feet.)

25. SPOKE.

26. Y. (In the first row the letters go up by 3, in the second row they go up by 4, in the last row they go up by 5.)

27. MOUSE. (All the others are seats: chair, stool, throne.)

28. AMID. (The first letter of the word in brackets is the second letter of the first word, the second is the first letter of the first word, the third is the second letter of the second word, the third is the first letter of the second word.)

29. A and I. (The word reads CHAMPION in an anti-clockwise direction.)

30. 3. (Square the numbers 8, 6, 4, 2 then add and subtract 1 from each alternately.)

31. 1. (Live dogs count +1, dead ones —1.)

32. POST.

33. MINUTE.

34. FISH. (All the others are parts of the body: nose, mouth, stomach, and hands.)

35. EDGE. (The first letter of the word in the brackets is the second letter of the first word, the second is the fifth letter of the first word, the third is the second letter of the second word, the fourth is the first letter of the second word.)

36. 2. (There are three positions: up, down, and sideways; 3 types of top; and 1, 2, or 3 lines at the bottom. Each of these occurs only once in each row and column.)

37. 2. (There are 1, 2, or 3 lines at the bottom of each figure; the crossbar is straight, bent upwards or downwards, and the balls to the right and to the left are either black, white, or shaded, independently of each other. Each feature only occurs once in each row or column, so that those not represented in the third row or column must appear in the missing figure.)

38. TEST. (The first letter of the word in the brackets is the first letter of the first word, the second is the second letter of the second word, the third is the third letter of the second word, the fourth is the fourth letter of the first word.)

39.

O
16

(In the number series, add 3, 4, and 5. In the letter series, take the third, fourth, and fifth letter following.)

40. —4. (Take the series: 8, 10, 12, 14, 16; add 1, 2, 3, etc.: 9, 12, 15, 18, 21; subtract 1^2, 2^2, 3^2, etc.: —1, —4, —9, —16, 25; 8, 8, 6, 2, —4.)

Test Five

1. 1. (There are three types of head and three positions for the arms.)

2. HER.

3. PIMPLE. (All the others are colours: indigo, black, white.)

4. 18. (The number in the tail is 3 times the difference between the numbers in the wings.)

5. 1. (There are black, white, and shaded rectangles on the right and left of each figure; each occurs only once in each row and column.)

6. 5. (There are two alternate series: 5, 4, 3, and 7, 6, 5.)

7. 4. (There are three types of loads to be carried, three types of shading for the front wheel, and three couplings.)

8. SAPS. (The first letter of the word in the brackets is the fifth letter of the first word, the second is the second letter of the first word, the third is the fourth letter of the second word, the fourth is the third letter of the second word.)

9. 1. (Adding the numbers on the left of the bracket and subtracting the sum of the numbers on the right of the bracket gives the number inside the bracket.)

10. WORMS. (All the others are writing instruments: pencil, quill, chalk.)

11. T. (The letters go up by 2, 3, 4, 5 steps.)

12.
8
7

(There are two series, alternating from numerator to denominator, each going up by 2.)

13. O and E. (The word reads FOREHEAD in an anti-clockwise direction.)

14. 1. (There are three types of boot, three different positions, three hair styles.)

15. 3. (The lines of the drawings in column 2 are taken away from those in column 1 to make those in column 3.)

16. AND.

17. 211. (Add the left- and right-hand numbers and divide by 3 to get the number in the brackets.)

18. 6. (To get the third number add the other two numbers and take away one.)

19. ARE.

20. 53. (Half the difference of the numbers outside the brackets gives the number inside the bracket.)

21. TOIL. (The first letter of the word in the brackets is the second letter of the second word, the second is the third letter of the second word, the third is the third letter of the first word, the fourth is the fourth letter of the first word.)

22. 63. (Cube the numbers 1, 2, 3, and 4 respectively, each time subtracting 1.)

23. HAROLD. (All the others are girls' names: Irma, Brigitte, Connie.)

24. 6. (There are three shapes of face and of ear; and three kinds of hats; each occurs only once in each row and column.)

25. GRAIN.

26. A. (Rows and columns give the same words and A is the only letter that will make a word.)

27. 131. (Add and subtract alternately the numbers 3, 9, 27, 81 respectively; i.e. treble each time.)

28. 1. (The ghosts have one, two, or three lines: one, two or, three wing feathers; and white, black, or shaded bottoms.)

29. BARS. (The first letter of the word in the brackets is the first letter of the first word, the second is the third letter of the first word, the third is the second letter of the second word, the fourth is the fifth letter of the second word.)

30. 3. (Circles outside the figure count plus, circles inside count minus. —3 + 4 = +1, so the answer is one circle outside the figure.)

31. CRAFT.

32. LOUSE. (All the others are furniture: carpet, desk, chair.)

33. E and E. (The word reads HELPLESS in a clockwise direction.)

34.

Q	(One series, alternating from the numerator of one square to the denominator of the next and so on, goes up by three letters each time; the other alternating series goes up by four each time.)
L	

35. SAND. (The first letter of the word in brackets is the last letter of the first word, the second is the second letter of the second word, the third is the third letter of the first word, the fourth is the last letter of the second word.)

36. LEAN.

37. PATS. (The first letter of the word in brackets is the last letter of the first word, the second is the third letter of the first word, the third is the last letter of the second word, the fourth is the third letter of the second word.)

38. 5. (There are three main shapes; inside each there are three small figures, each of which can be in one of three positions; one of them is black. Each feature only occurs once in each row or column.)

39. 4. (The figure in the third column is made up of the lines from the figures in the first two columns which are not in common to both.)

40.

4
6

(There are two series, each alternating from the numerator of one fraction to the denominator of the next. One decreases by 1 starting with 9; the other decreases by 1, starting with 5, but this time is squared.)

Verbal Ability

1. NOVEL.

2. LAD.

3. STOMACH. (All the others are ball games: football, cricket, and tennis.)

4. ICK.

5. PRESS.

6. END.

7. MILTON. (All the others are singers: Crosby, Sinatra, and Presley.)

8. BLACK.

9. MATE.

10. TENT.

11. GARDEN. (All the others are forms of communication: post, radio, phone.)

12. SHOE.

13. IN.

14. SLIT.

15. CHERRIES. (All the other words have an A in them: carrots, dates, apples, and cabbages.)

16. EAR.

17. RIP.

18. CHAIR. (All the others are flowers: peony, poppy, buttercup, tulip.)

19. AIL.

20. FINE.

21. ON.

22. WALNUT. (All the others are breeds of dog: terrier, alsatian, and boxer.)

23. FIRE.

24. EEP.

25. RING.

26. FLORIDA. (All the others are English counties: Surrey, Essex, Cornwall.)

27. PRESS.

28. CORN.

29. BELGRADE. (The others are Cairo, Tokio, and Toronto.)

30. ENT.

31. ING.

32. FORM.

33. STRING.

34. WHALE. (All the others are birds: eagle, sparrow, and lark.)

35. UMP.

36. TAR.

37. EINSTEIN. (All the others are famous as writers: Dickens, Wells, Defoe, Swift.)

38. BILL.

39. INT.

40. NICK.

41. LINE.

42. TELEVISION. (All the others are insects: mosquito, gnat, termite.)

43. FRESH.

44. FEND.

45. OCK.

46. SEMAPHORE. (All the others are animals: goat, horse, beaver.)

47. IPS.

48. RUST.

49. ARK.

50. VIOLIN. (All the others are relatives: brother, sister, aunt, and mother.)

Numerical Ability

1. 48. (Add 2, 4, 8, and finally 16.)

2. 24. (Going anti-clockwise, the numbers go up by 2, 3, 4, 5, 6.)

3. 80. (Subtract 33 from each number.)

4. 5. (Arms pointing upwards are added and arms pointing downwards are subtracted, to give the number on the head.)

5. 18. (There are two alternating series, one ascending by 4 steps, the other by 3 steps.)

6. 154. (Add numbers outside the brackets and multiply by 2.)

7. 3. (Take the difference between numbers in first two columns and divide by 2.)

8. 86. (Double the number and then subtract 1, 2, 3, and 4.)

9. 333. (Subtract the left-hand number from the right-hand number to get the number in the brackets.)

10. 35. (The series goes up by 1, 2, 4, 8, and 16 steps.)

11. 5. (The number in the head is half the sum of the numbers in the feet.)

12. 37. (Double each term and subtract 5 to get the next number.)

13. 7. (Numbers in the third column are half the sum of numbers in the other two columns.)

14. 33. (The series descends by 16, 8, 4, 2, and 1 steps.)

15. 3. (Going round the square clockwise, multiply by 3.)

16. 14. (Add the numbers outside the brackets and divide by 50 to get the number inside.)

17. 6. (There are two alternating series; one descends by 3, the other by 2.)

18. 4. (Each row adds up to 14.)

19. 18. (Doubling each term and subtracting 10 gives the next.)

20. 3. (The numbers go down by equal steps, 3 in the first row, 2 in the second, and 3 in the third.)

21. 18. (The numbers are twice those in the diagonally opposite sections.)

22. 232. (Subtract the left-hand side from the right-hand side and double the answer.)

23. 21. (The numbers go up by 2, 4, 6, and 8 intervals.)

24. 480. (The number inside the brackets is twice the product of the numbers outside the brackets.)

25. 2. (The third column is twice the difference between the first and second.)

26. 19. (There are two series, one goes up in 3, 4, and 5 steps, the other goes down in 2 and 3 steps.)

27. 3. (Subtract the sum of the second and fourth paws from the sum of the second and third paws to get the number on the top of the tail.)

28. 77. (The number in the brackets is half the product of the numbers outside the brackets.)

29. 7. (Halve each number and take away two to get the next term.)

30. 61. (Add twice the difference between successive numbers to get the next one. Thus $5 - 1 = 4$; $2 \times 4 = 8$; $8 + 5 = 13$; etc.)

31. 11. (Double each number and add one to get the number in the opposite sector.)

32. 46. (Add one to each number and then double to get the next number.)

33. 24. (The series increases by 3, 5, 7, and 9.)

34. 5. (There are two alternating series. One going up by 2 each time, the other going down by 1 each time.)

35. 518. (The number inside the brackets is twice the difference between the numbers outside the brackets.)

36. 3. (Subtract the sum of the numbers on the legs from the sum of the numbers on the arms to give the number on the head.)

37. 19. (There are two alternating series; one ascending by 5, the other ascending by 4.)

38. 152. (Double each number and add 2, 3, 4, 5, and 6.)

39. 40. (The numbers in the second column are formed by taking those in the first, doubling them, and adding 1; those in the third by taking those in the second, doubling them, and adding 2. Thus $(2 \times 19) + 2 = 40$.)

40.

20
26

(The numerator numbers increase by 3, 4, 5, and then 6 steps, while the denominator numbers increase by 4, 5, 6, and 7 steps.)

41. 66. (Double each preceding number, going in a clockwise direction, and subtract 2.)

42. 179. (Each figure is obtained by doubling the preceding one and adding 1, 3, 5, 7, and finally 9.)

43. 64. (Numbers and their squares are in diagonal sectors.)

44. 111. (The number inside the brackets is half the difference of the numbers outside the brackets.)

45. 297. (The difference is doubled each time and is alternately added and subtracted from successive numbers.)

46. 6. (There are two alternating series. Each one is squared and a constant two added.

The first is :   0   3   6   9,

square   :   0   9 36 81,

add 2   :   2 11 38 83.

The second is: 5   4   3   hence 2,

square   : 25 16   9   hence 4,

add 2   : 27 18 11   hence 6.)

47. 55 and 100. (The number required behind the brackets is the square of that in front of it. The number inside the brackets is half the sum of the numbers outside the brackets.)

48. 91. (Add 1 to the first number $(7 + 1 = 8)$, then add the sum to the second number $(8 + 19 = 27)$ and so on till you get: $(125+$ the missing number $= ?)$

The sums so far obtained make the series 1, 8, 27, 64, 125, which are the cubes of numbers 1, 2, 3, 4, and 5. To complete the series, therefore, take the cube of 6 $(= 216)$.

So that you get $(125 + ? = 216)$ and the answer is 91.)

49. 581. (Start with the series: 0   2   4   6   hence 8,

multiply by 3   : 0   6 12 18   hence 24,

square   : 0 36 144 324   hence 576,

add 5   : 5 41 149 329   hence 581.)

50. 6. (Add all numbers inside the corners of the triangles and subtract those outside the triangle; this gives the number in the circle.)

Visuo-Spatial Ability

1. 4. (All the other drawings can be turned upside down without making any difference.)

2. 3. (All the other figures can be rotated into each other.)

3. 2. (All the other figures can be rotated into each other.)

4. 4. (The figure is turned through an angle of 90 degrees anti-clockwise each time, except for number 4 which goes clockwise.)

5. 1. (All the other figures can be rotated into each other.)

6. 4. (The figure is turned through an angle of 90 degrees anti-clockwise each time, except for number 4 which goes clockwise.)

7. 4. (All the other figures can be rotated into each other.)

8. 1. (The main figure is turned over, and the little circle is transferred to the other side.)

9. 4. (All the other figures can be rotated into each other in the plane of the paper.)

10. 5. (All the other figures can be rotated into each other.)

11. 3. (The other three show a *right* hand rotated into various positions; 3 is a *left* hand!)

12. 3. (The figure rotates anti-clockwise through half a quarter turn, but the black shading rotates one position further, except in 3, which is therefore the odd man out.)

13. 2. (All the other figures can be rotated into each other.)

14. 1. (All the other figures can be rotated into each other.)

15. 4. (All the other figures can be rotated into each other.)

16. 5. (The whole set of 4 circles is turned through an angle of 90 degrees each time. In 5 the cross and X have in addition changed places; in all other figures the cross is in the same row as the black circle.)

17. 3. (All the other figures can be rotated into each other.)

18. 5. (All the other figures can be rotated into each other.)

19. 2. (All the other figures can be rotated into each other.)

20. 6. (All the other figures can be rotated into each other.)

21. 5. (1 and 3, and 2 and 4, are pairs; they can be rotated into each other by a quarter turn. 5 cannot be rotated so because the cross and circle inside it would be in the wrong place.)

22. 1. (All the other figures can be rotated into each other.)

23. 4. (The black, white, and shaded portions rotate positions anti-clockwise; in 4 the shaded and white portions are in the wrong positions.)

24. 4. (All the other figures can be rotated into each other.)

25. 4. (All the other figures can be rotated into each other.)

26. 3. (1 and 4 are a pair, so are 2 and 5. In each pair the black and the shaded portion change places. 3 has the shading going the wrong way.)

27. 5. (All the other figures can be rotated into each other.)

28. 2. (Shading is transferred from outer figures to inner figures and vice versa; position (upright or horizontal) remains constant.)

29. 3. (All the other figures can be rotated into each other.)

30. 3. (All the other figures can be rotated into each other.)

31. 3. (The main figure rotates clockwise, the arrow anti-clockwise.)

32. 5. (All the other figures can be rotated into each other.)

33. 2 and 5. (The other four figures can be rotated into each other; 2 and 5 cannot.)

34. 2. (The main figure is turned anti-clockwise through 90 degrees together with the small side figures which are then interchanged; i.e. those at the top go to the bottom, those at the bottom go to the top.)

35. 1 and 2. (All the other figures can be rotated into each other.)

36. 3. (Each of the other drawings follows the rule that the whole drawing is rotated through 90 degrees each time; in figure 3 the shading goes the wrong way.)

37. 3. (The main figure is turned through 180 degrees (upside down), the three black bands become two, and the three small figures move anti-clockwise by one position.)

38. 2. (What is round in the first figure becomes square; what is pointing upwards points downwards.)

39. 3 and 6. (The other five figures can be rotated into each other.)

40. 1, 3, and 6. (The other four can be rotated into each other.)

41. 2, 3, and 7. (The other four can be rotated into each other.)

42. 1 and 4. (The other figures can be rotated into each other.)

43. 8. (All the other figures can be rotated into each other.)

44. 3. (The bottom figure and the top figure change places; the figure inside the top one remains, but the shading inside the bottom one changes places with the unshaded part. The scrawls at the right and left of the main figure change places.)

45. 1, 6, and 7. (The other five can be rotated into each other.)

46. 7. (All the other figures can be rotated into each other.)

47. 2, 6, and 7. (The other six figures can be rotated into each other.)

48. 1, 6, and 8. (All the other six figures can be rotated into each other.)

49. 5, 6, and 8. (The other six figures can be rotated into each other.)

50. 6. (All the other figures can be rotated into each other.)

Limbering Up for Intellectual Giants I

1.

    (Take the numbers 2, 3, 4, 5, and 6. To get the top number in each domino, square each and subtract 1, 2, 3, 4, and 5. To get the bottom number, take the cube and subtract the top number.)

2. INSOLUBLE. (Giving the vowels numbers: A = 1, E = 2, I = 3, O = 4, U = 5. Add these in each word, and each pair must be equal.

    $$\left.\begin{array}{l} \text{i.e. } 5 + 5 + 5 + 1 = 16 \\ 5 + 2 + 4 + 2 + 3 = 16 \end{array}\right\}$$

    $$\left.\begin{array}{l} 5 + 5 + 1 + 3 = 14 \\ \text{thus } 3 + 4 + 5 + 2 = 14 \end{array}\right\} \quad \begin{array}{l} \text{The vowels in the} \\ \text{other words do not} \\ \text{add up to 14.)} \end{array}$$

3. 238. (Divide the differences between the consecutive numbers by 3 and add to the previous term to get the next number.)

4. 56. (Give the letters their numbers in the alphabet, square each and add these squares. Subtract these sums to get the answer.

    i.e. GIBE — FADE
    (7925) — (6145)
    square (49 + 81 + 4 + 25) — (36 + 1 + 16 + 25)
    sum 159 — 78 = 81
    etc.)

5. 84. (There are two series. One gives the vowels the following values: A = 1, E = 2, I = 3, O = 4, U = 5. The other is the numbers of the letters (other than vowels) in the alphabet in reverse. Thus B = 25, C = 24, to Z = 1.)

6. ACTOR. (Substitute numbers for letters, alternately taking A as 1, B as 2 etc., and Z as 1, Y as 2 etc. LOUSE adds up to 58, SCALP to 75, HOUND to 58, and only ACTOR of the other words adds up to 75.)

7. 25. (Take the first number, multiply by 2, and subtract 4; then multiply by 3 and subtract 5; then multiply by 4 and subtract 6 etc.)

8. 89. (The letters are given their corresponding numbers in the alphabet, alternating with their numbers in the reversed alphabet (i.e. Z = 1 to A = 26). Starting with the reversed alphabet, G = 20, then the ordinary alphabet E = 5 etc. to total 95.)

9. X. (B is the second letter of the alphabet; multiply 2 by 3 and then subtract 3; this gives 3. C is the third letter of the alphabet: multiply 3 by 3, and subtract 4; this gives 5. E is the fifth letter of the alphabet, etc.)

10. OLD. (H is the eighth letter of the alphabet, and S is the eighth letter of the alphabet written backwards. Similarly all the other letters in each pair of words correspond.)

11. 32. (Square numbers 0, 1, 2, 3, 4 respectively, each time multiplying by 2.
thus: $0^2 \times 2 = 0$
$1^2 \times 2 = 2$
$2^2 \times 2 = 8$
$3^2 \times 2 = 18$
$4^2 \times 2 = 32$)

12. 11. (Take the sentence GOD SAVE THE QUEEN. Give each letter its appropriate number in the alphabet and add the numbers for each word, dividing by the number of letters in the word.

$$\text{Thus GOD} = \frac{7 + 15 + 4}{3} = \frac{26}{3} = 8\frac{2}{3}$$

$$\text{and THE} = \frac{20 + 8 + 5}{3} = \frac{33}{3} = 11.)$$

13. 34. *Easy.* Each number is formed by subtracting the succeeding one from the next one: $34 - 21 = 13$, hence the missing one is 34.

Difficult. The square of any number is differed by 1 from the product of the numbers to the right and left of it. $21^2 = 441$; $13 \times 34 = 442$.)

14. 47. (Give each letter its appropriate number in the alphabet, and multiply by the number denoting its position in the word. i.e. 1, 2, 3, or 4.)

15. 98.

(Take the series:	8	10	12	14	16
Square each:	64	100	144	196	256
Divide by 2:	32	50	72	98	128
Subtract 30:	2	20	42	68	98.)

16. 87. There are two series. One is A = 5, E = 4, I = 3, O = 2, U = 1; the other is the ordinary number the letter (other than vowels) has in the alphabet. The two series are combined and then the letters added. e.g. REWARDED = 18 + 4 + 23 + 5 + 18 + 4 + 4 + 4 = 80.)

17. CONSCIOUSLY. (Coding vowels A = 5, E = 4, I = 3, O = 2, U = 1. Add the numerical values of the vowels in each word. All come to 18, except those in CONSCIOUSLY which come to 8.)

18. 2. (The letters stand for numbers: A = 4, B = 9, C = 1, D = 5, E = 2, F = 7, G = 8, H = 3, I = 6.)

19. CRUISING. (Take the five vowels, and call A = 1, E = 2, I = 3, O = 4, U = 5. Add up the values of the vowels in the words, and you get: 9 is to 9 as 11 is to ? Only CRUISING adds up to 11.)

20. 147 4 172 7. (Give the letters of the alphabet the usual numbers, i.e. A = 1 to Z = 26. The sentence reads: MARY HAD A LITTLE LAMB. The numbers of the letters, however, are each squared and a constant 3 is added each time. i.e. MARY = $(13^2 + 3)$ $1^2 + 3$ $18^2 + 3$ $25^2 + 3$
= 169 + 3   1 + 3   324 + 3   625 + 3
= 172   4   327   628
etc.)

Limbering Up for Intellectual Giants II

1. 343. (Multiply each number by the preceding one and divide by 2.)

2. 39. (Take material values of letters going up and down the alphabet alternately.)

3. 88. (Multiply each number by 3, and subtract 14. $3 \times 34 = 102$, $102 - 14 = 88$.)

4. 9. (Count number of letters in word and add one to get number.)

5. MIKE. (The letters in the male names have their numerical value in the alphabet; those in the female names with alphabet reversed (i.e. Z = 1, Y = 2, etc.) EVE — ADAM = 30, JOAN — MIKE = 30.)

6. PUMPERNICKEL. (The letters are given their appropriate numbers, using the alphabet forwards and then backwards alternately (P = 16th forwards, U = 6th backwards, etc.). PASTICHE and PESTILENCE add up to 131, and only PUMPERNICKEL in the others also does so.)

7. X. (Take the number corresponding to those letters in the inverted alphabet, i.e. 22, 13, 8, 5. Each is derived from the preceding one by adding 4, 3, 2, and then 1, and halving: (22 + 4 = 26, 26 ÷ 2 = 13); (5 + 1 = 6, 6 ÷ 2 = 3). The third letter in the inverted alphabet is X.)

8. 44. (Give letters the appropriate numbers in the alphabet; add together each alternate letter, starting with the first one.)

9. GUT. (The two consonants in the other words are an equal number of letters removed from the vowel in the middle; e.g. J is five letters before O, and T is five letters behind.)

10. 13. (Give appropriate numbers to the letters: GIRL (5267) and BOY (931). POOR (4336) is the first minus the second. 20 is the sum of the figures in girl, and 13 is the sum of the figures in boy.)

11. 179. (Take a series of numbers starting with 1, where each is formed by multiplying the previous one by 3, e.g. 1, 3, 9, 27, 81, etc. Take another series starting with 2 and made up by multiplying by 2 i.e. 2, 4, 8, 16, 32, etc. Subtract the latter from the former and you get the series given here. Thus 243 — 64 = 179.)

12. HARLOT. (The number of letters in the alphabet between the first and last letters of each word is twice that of the letters in the word between first and last plus one.

    Thus in CRANK there are 3 letters between C and K. Twice 3 plus one is 7, and there are seven letters between C and K in the alphabet (DEFGHIJ). Harlot is the odd man out.)

13. PETROL. (In each word substitute numbers for letters, counting alternately from the beginning or the end of the alphabet. Only PETROL completes the equation properly.)

14. 0. (To get the second number in each row, take the third power of the first, and subtract the first number, e.g. $3^3 = 27$, $27 - 3 = 24$. To get the third number, divide the second number by 12, and then square it.)

15. TON. (In all the other words the consonants are next to each other in the alphabet: S and R, M and N, F and G, H and G.)

16. X. (Letters are set equal to a certain number $Z = 1$, $X = 2$, $V = 3$, $T = 4$, $R = 5$, $P = 6$, $N = 7$, $L = 8$, and $J = 9$. The letters go backwards in the alphabet, skipping one letter each time.)

17. 0. (Give each letter its number in the alphabet, ordinarily and in reversed order alternately, and sum for each word.)

18. 441. (Multiply each number by the last figure in that number to get the next term.)

19. 4/3. (Multiply two successive numbers and divide by 1, 2, 3, and 4 respectively to get the next term:

$$\left(\frac{\frac{1}{3} \times 3}{1}\right) \quad \left(\frac{3 \times 4}{2}\right) \quad \left(\frac{4 \times 6}{3}\right) \quad \left(\frac{6 \times 8}{4}\right)$$

20. 1. (Give the vowels the following values: $A = 0$, $E = 1$, $I = 2$, $O = 3$, $U = 4$. Adding these in each name gives the number of children. MAUD $= 0 + 4 = 4$; JOHN $= 3$ etc.)

Transforming Scores into I.Q.s

To find your I.Q., enter your score on the base line of the appropriate graph on the next three pages. Draw a line straight up until it meets the diagonal line; the point on the vertical line corresponding to this gives your I.Q. The scores are most accurate between I.Q.s of 100 and 130; beyond these limits too much reliance should not be placed upon them.

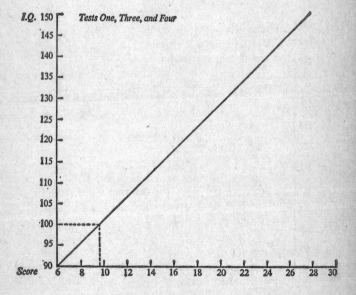

Tests One, Three, and Four

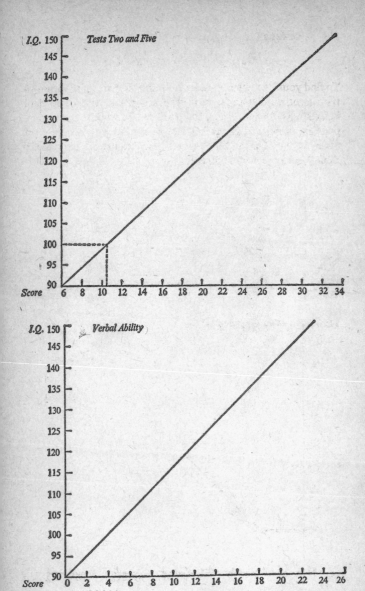

I.Q. Tests Two and Five

Score

I.Q. Verbal Ability

Score

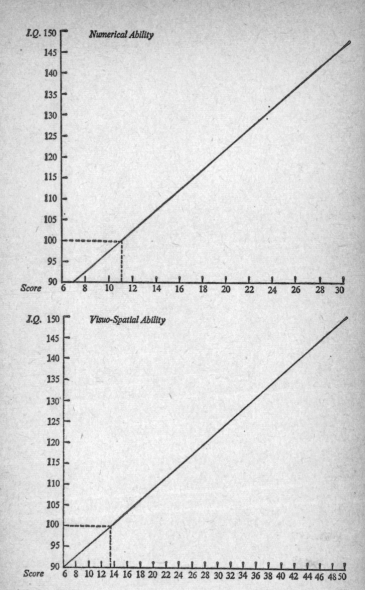